CARRY MY BONES

A NOVEL BY

J. WES YODER

D1570418

CARRY MY BONES

A NOVEL BY

J. WES YODER

MACADAM CAGE

MacAdam/Cage
155 Sansome Street, Suite 550
San Francisco, CA 94104
www.macadamcage.com

Library of Congress Cataloging-in-Publication Data

Yoder, J. Wes, 1979–
  Carry my bones / by J. Wes Yoder.
    p. cm.
  ISBN 1-59692-175-7 (alk. paper)
  1. Sculptors—Fiction. 2. Fugitives from justice—Fiction. 3. Alabama—Fiction.
I. Title.
  PS3625.O338C37 2006
  813'.6—dc22

                                                          2006000700

Paperback edition: June 2007
ISBN 978-1-59692-221-1

Manufactured in the United States of America.
10 9 8 7 6 5 4 3 2 1

Jacket painting by Emily Leonard.
Book and jacket design by Dorothy Carico Smith.

For Jennifer Joy

"Meanwhile we groan."

—*St. Paul*

PART ONE

1.

JOHN FREDERICK USED TO SAY THAT EVERYBODY OUT THERE HAS A PROBLEM with time. They all got the wrong amount, and the more they think about it, the less it behaves. He said time wasn't a thing we could handle because, for God, a day is a thousand years, and a thousand years is a day, but a person can't have it both ways at once. So there's time slipping through fingers that want to hold it, and there's time caking feet that want to run free of it, and a clock ticking can only make a grown man uncomfortable. But time never troubled me. The sun rising couldn't order my life, and there was nothing new about another year. I kicked my feet out in front of me and I wished for nothing. But then, during two days in Birmingham, I lost all of that. Off in the distance of every resurrection stood death, and its shadow was wide and crept like an hour hand. So now I turn away and remember the spring as if we never left it. The smell of honeysuckle and snakes. The college football radio show. The days eating away at the nights. In that hand it is a pot of coffee. Still in the other it is an old and shrinking burn. Because when I think about the way we were, and all the things we've lost and taken, and all the ground we covered and how it covered part of us, it seems that I have lived most of my life in the past six months.

Back then, I'd sit with Gid in the bed of his truck and listen to the radio show. He'd empty a beer, hand me the can, and start about his season tickets. The payment was due and his wife wouldn't lend him the money. And of all the years for her to pull this. He had held tickets for thirty-one average seasons, and now a lot of people were saying it was Auburn's year to win it all. So there was Gid in a lawn chair in the truck bed, trying to figure something. His hands would be red with clay, and when he scratched his face the sweat ran muddy down his jaw.

"It's no good, Junior," he'd say.

And I'd say, "Yeah, it's bad."

And that's how we were then. That was a thing to worry about.

———

The papers will say that our story began one Tuesday in September. But the papers think too much of time. Things had started changing in the spring, around the day when Gid's transmission fell. He was on the way to town to see a man about some money when it happened, and he took it the last dozen miles in first gear. During that hour, bumping along the shoulder, he thought it was perfect that everyone should be passing him by. That's the thing he had felt for a long time, and now he could lean back and watch it. He called me from the auto shop and told me that he had begged the mechanic for a gentleman's loan. He had played football with the boy in high school, they had raised some hell, and there he was, begging. But he said it was just as well. He said it was like that for a man who couldn't fix his own shit.

I understood it to be the first time he hadn't crossed two counties to get a vehicle serviced where he could be sure that no one would know him. And I hung up the phone realizing he'd finally spoken a thing he'd been trying to ignore: that he had a pair of rich man's hands.

Not that naming a fear will make it untrue. For Gid, one admission led to another, and things got muddier. So it wasn't only football and money to stir him up. Or that his hands wanted to make art and were no good for doing real work. It was the woman he had married and all the reasons it had gotten bad. He'd only ever bragged on her.

In the weeks after I noticed that his art improved, his focus sharpened by shame. But he was making uglier things. Then, one afternoon, while having some trouble fashioning the likeness of a rat on a jug, he started pedaling the wheel. He got it going fast and held his wet palm there until the animal was gone. The wheel slowed and stopped and so did his mutter. And his lips twisted and stretched and grinned with that strange and sudden intoxication of realized defeat, or just the realization that failure can be called something nobler. It was a beaten man's smile, and he wasn't looking at anything. He fetched a screwdriver, climbed in the cab where the radio show was talking, and removed the rack with the guns that he'd often cleaned and hardly fired. And he spun the dial to a news program.

I mostly kept in the woods after that. I'd go see John Frederick and we'd sit until the shadows were long and gray and weak. And every time I'd come back I'd be expecting Gid to have gone back to liquor. But then another thing happened.

"Junior," he said. I was napping after lunch. He was in his chair by the TV. "Wake up, Junior, and hear this. Our governor has just tried to dupe us. He said we're in a money crisis and we all got to pay our part, like a tithe. But that's not the thing about it. He said we get to vote on it. We get to decide if he can have our dollars. Don't that seem like telling someone you're gonna hit them before you do? No. It's worse than that. That's like telling someone to hit their own self."

He was pacing in the kitchen. He opened and slammed some cabinets. And for the rest of the afternoon he said the same thing.

But I knew that Gid didn't care about the referendum. When he did manage to sell some pottery, he sold it for cash. To him taxes were like some stranger's crippled limp; it was sad that a person should have to bear up under something like that, and it reminded him that he was fine. But I also knew why he was huffing. Just spot anyone hoisting a protest banner, anyone making a hobby of hate, and you've found a man who's defected from the war in his own head. So being a Democrat by birth who distrusted liberals, and never one to cheer for an underdog, Gid would oppose the Republican governor, who was behaving less than conservative. He would try to keep himself worked up, remembering all the relatives before him who got to fight in real wars.

For all that was going on with him, he didn't sound too different from anybody else. The whole state was riled. The governor was on the TV every night looking like he would cry. He was saying that thousands of teachers would be cut from schools if the people voted no, and that there wouldn't be any money to keep children away from parents who beat them, and that it was shameful that a state university should be praised for having the best football squad in the country when the state's health care and roads had fallen apart.

Pastors went on the radio to say that Montgomery had lost sight of morality. They said that the government wasn't accountable for the money they already had, so why should it pass the plate for more?

And of course there were the newspapers. But this time they were rallying for a Republican. They said that people had a responsibility to their children and grandchildren to vote yes. They said that even after the increase, Alabamians would remain some of the lowest-taxed people in the country, and that poorer families would pay even less than they already did. They drew sketches of prosperity: houses with no shutters missing, schoolrooms with no children sharing a desk, highways smooth and long with no trash or dead animals on the side. I kept looking for some fine print that said, "paid advertisement."

———

It was May when Gid sculpted his life-size, seated statue of the governor. It took him two weeks to do it, and a pile of mud, and if he hadn't been so beaten up before he started, I would have told him he was wasting his time. He painted on a gray suit with a white pencil stripe and red necktie and fired it in three pieces. Then he shined it, as he did every piece, with an egg on a rag. The next week he showed it at the art festival in Columbus on the other side of the river. It was Georgia there. It shouldn't have mattered. But people lined up all weekend to get their pictures taken with the thing, and to drop quarters in the governor's mouth. They rattled inside him for a bit, then pinged into a metal toilet Gid had salvaged from the old county jail. There was a campaign button on the lapel that said, "I'm the dollar defecator." It won a prize.

Gid brought home a few buckets of quarters on Sunday. I sat in the truck bed and stuffed them into rolls while he had a beer and looked at himself on the newspapers.

"Damn, Junior. I forgot to take off my hat," he said. "You can't see my eyes."

"You already said that," I said. "I think you look beautiful."

"I'll drown you." He looked through the trees to the house. "We'll get rich off this."

"Richer," I said.

"I sold more face mugs than last year by triple. And you know what that means. I'm done kissing Georgia ass to get in the show. They already told me I could have a better spot next time. Get me away from all the quilting ladies and kids' crafts."

He slicked the sweat on his forehead back through his hair. He was fighting a smile.

"It was something," he said. "All them artists that would never talk to me were coming around. Them with the fancy tents and the framed articles about themselves. But they couldn't even see much because I had the people lined up all across the path. And them old black boys were coming, you know the kind. Them who have killed and murdered probably, and who paint with their muddy fingers picture after picture of a woman's privates, and who the dealers from Chicago and San Francisco all gather around and call precious, well they were coming too. They were chewing their cigarettes like they do and looking at all the girls in my line."

"Did you sell that one of the buzzard at the pulpit?" I asked.

"This woman broke it when we were sitting around last night. She was drinking sweet wine and she tripped over the tent stake."

"Did she pay for it?"

"I made her kiss me for a photograph."

"Yeah?" I said. "How'd she look?"

He slapped a mosquito on his wrist, rubbed the blood into the itch, then looked at the house for a while.

"Can you glue it back?" I asked.

It was a while before he spoke. He kept looking past the trees.

"She don't even come out to see it," he said. "She's in there talking to her sister."

I kept working while he told me what it was like to come home to a wife who wouldn't get off the telephone when you opened the door. He said he'd rather be cussed than ignored. Take a dog, he said. It's not the one you beat too hard that bites a child on the face. It's the one you never mind. And you wonder how that calm animal could have violence inside.

He climbed down and went to his wheel. He dropped a piece of clay there, dipped his hands in the water bucket, and beat the stuff. I went for a walk.

When I made it through the woods, John Frederick wasn't home. So I lay on the ramp to his place and watched the clouds. I was glad for Gid. Maybe he had been cracking when he quit everything to make pottery, but he had stuck with it. He did it the old way, with a pedal wheel and river mud. His hands were bad. He couldn't feel much, so he had spent a few years just trying to get the shapes right. Now he had found a style that suited him, and he said he could finally make the things he saw in his head. It was good that he should get a little praise for his governor. He had waited plenty long to get inside the world of outsider art.

I woke up when John Frederick pulled up. He stopped under the tree and cut the motor. I peeked at him just sitting there behind the wheel, talking at his windshield, like I've seen him do for an hour or more. When he got out, I faked sleep.

"Okay, yeah," he said. "Okay. I see you now but I don't at first."

He was at my feet. I sat up and tied his shoe.

"You not sick are you? I'll put you in my bed."

"Just resting."

"I thought maybe you step on Mr. Scorpion. I did."

He had been working over at the Fishers of Men A.M.E. Dirt cuffed his pants and there was dried foam at the corners of his mouth. Every year he planted the churchyard in turnips. Then he gave them away in paper sacks each Sunday in August.

"Let me tell you something," he said, and he took my wrist. "If a turnip grow, it's 'cause God told him to. And if a man die, it's 'cause God told him to go ahead and die. Ain't that true? It is. No one chooses the time. Eben if you do it to yourself, you're not choosing."

In the darkness of his face his eyes set yellow, and they were prone to glow like wished coins in a silt creek. He held them over the field towards the scum pond and he raked the back of his fingers against some white stubble. Then he turned back quick.

"God has not said to me, 'Mr. John, it's time you die.' Not yet. I ask him to let me go on till I'm one hundred and ten. He might not do it. But he might. Moses went to one hundred and twenty."

A while later, when I put my hand on his shoulder, he jumped. I handed him a roll of quarters.

"I do thank you," he said. "Yes sir."

I walked behind the trailer and into the trees. The woods were sticky, and as I went along the deer path, I thought of the old man.

He hoped that one of these years they would let him be "of the service." He wanted a seat on the deacon bench. But I got the feeling it would never happen. That even his people thought he was off. It didn't matter much. As long as he could garden there and as long as the turnips charmed the widows.

The woods were getting quiet. The birds were bedding up and the tree frogs hadn't started. I took a stick and tapped the trees I passed. Heat lightning grumbled a long way off and I started running. I ducked branches and slipped past thorns until I hopped the place where a tree had mashed the fence and landed in the field. My breath came heavy, the light was warm, and I didn't know why I had run.

I pulled my shoes off in the mudroom and checked my socks for ticks. Gid was watching the Braves.

"Javy's got three strikeouts," he said. "Twice looking."

I mentioned that they were winning 8 to 3 and were toting the best record in baseball.

"Yeah. That's right. But they'll fold in October," he said. "Just watch. They're too fat and their wives are too pretty."

Robyn had gone to a friend's to play gin rummy. She would come home late and leave Gid asleep in his chair. I don't like watching baseball before fall, so I took a can of pickles and a bag of chips to my room and fell asleep a while later reading Cabelo's catalog.

2.

Invitations to Vote-No rallies started coming steady. They were for family reunions and church cookouts and county fairs. The letters were stacked on the counter by the telephone. One went like this:

Dear Sir:

The referendum is going to make us all go broke. The state can't figure out how to manage their money, so they want more to waste. The governor wants a raise. Republicans.

We in Wolf Valley will not stand for it. We are going to help get the word out. My name is Cynthia Blaylock. I am the fire chief of the state's only all-female volunteer fire department. We would like to invite you and your statue of our embarrassing governor to our Stop the Stealing get-together, on Sunday, June 8. We think you will be able to help the people in Wolf Valley understand the governor's plan. It's bunk.

Our gathering begins at 3:30. Please call if you can come. You can stay in the firehouse if the evening goes late. Directions are on the back.

United in Justice,
Cynthia

Robyn found that one and put it in her purse. But for the most part, Gid spent the summer crisscrossing the state. His plan was simple. He told people that all of their quarters would go to one of the big organizations fighting for the cause. They added up.

With Gid gone it was just me and Robyn and her cat. When Robyn wasn't working, she was playing cards somewhere. She left me napkins every morning by the coffeepot.

You need to cut the yard. He called and said he won't be back till Sunday. The grass is embarrassing. You need to watch it doesn't get so tall. Thanks, R.

So I'd do some chore late in the morning, some thing that would spare her a lot of shame if, for the first time in years, anyone came down the driveway. Like spraying for silverfish. She had me do it every week. And the only silverfish I have ever seen is the drawing on the chemical bottle. On those days I'd hit a few baseboards, then her underwear drawer and her cat. I liked having the house to myself. I'd make a tomato sandwich every afternoon and take a nap. Then I'd walk to John Frederick's.

"Last night I awoke and a lightning bug was going around my bed," he said one day. "She was going around and around like this and flashing her butt and I said, 'You are pretty but this is my bed. Yes sir.' And when she came by me, I grabbed her like this and rubbed her butt down my arm like this and do you know my arm glow till morning."

He wanted to go riding around. So we drove that mile to the Green Store. It was the only place we'd ever stop. I went in and got a Dr. Pepper for me and a milk for the old man. And we sat in the car for a long time while the sun baked the big brown hood.

"What do you think about that one?" he asked.

There was a door-shaped woman at the diesel pump.

"Not too bad."

"That's right," he said. "A sight."

John Frederick liked all women. If their hair was big, he called it a crown. If they had a limp, he called it a gait. He said, "How you do," to any woman that walked close to his window and he didn't care if they ignored him.

That day we saw the only two who ever cared to talk to us. Verner Nail was a big widow from the Fishers of Men. She came out with a paper bag of seeds in one hand and an afternoon paper in the other.

"I can't get nothin' to grow this year," she said. "The deers eat it all up at night and my old dog is too deaf to hear. Gonna get me a pup, John Frederick. Keep them animals away from my food."

He held her hands together, cupped them, and said she could take some from his garden.

The other girl called herself Sweet Pants. She pulled up a while later in her old convertible, sort of jumped and fell over her door, and leaned her head in my window.

"Hello boys," she said. "Boys and gentlemen. Y'all finding any trouble today?"

John Frederick blushed. "No ma'am."

"Me neither. That's why I make my own. I mix it in an old washing machine and I use a lot of sugar."

It had taken me a long time to be able to look at her. Her jeans were always sliding down and she had a scar on her hip that hadn't closed up right. And her teeth were rotten. I guess she got her name from her job. She parked her car down near the bridge and sold sweet potatoes out of her backseat.

After she had driven off, John Frederick held his finger in front of his face. It quivered there like a candle, and he said, "Let me tell you something. Women, listen to me, are one of two things in this world that has any power. You know what the other is? The Holy Spirit. That's right. And if one of them don't move you, you either sick or dead. That's what you been needing to know."

He dozed for a while then. The milk was on his lap, unopened and hot. In all the years of sitting there I never saw him take a sip. Anyway, I was sweating against the seat, trying to figure how close I was to dead. And I may have slept a little too, because I didn't notice the man who opened the icebox there in front of our fender. But I saw him lean against it, kind of slide down the side of it until he was sitting on the gravel with his chin on his chest. A crowd gathered quick. It woke John Frederick and made him nervous, so he backed us out and drove on home. On the way he asked me if the man had a heart attack. I said I thought so.

"Nooo," he said. "I bet he seen a dead animal in there. A cat skinned or a possum maybe."

Later, as I was kicking through the high grass, I saw Gid's truck by the shed. He had shown up at the store after us, and he told me that a nine-year-old boy had frozen to death.

"I didn't see him, and that's fine," he said. "They had him all covered up. But Snag Holland told me the boy was blue as bunny blood. They think he had been in there since last night. Horace Green said he sold two bags of ice this morning to two different people. But neither of them seen the boy. It's like their heads couldn't believe their eyes."

I helped him wrap some pottery in newspaper. He'd been selling a lot at the rallies and he was only dropping in for another load. He had gotten rid of all the bigger, expensive pieces and all that was left were some coffee mugs with the broken-tile teeth and marble eyes. I climbed up in the bed to load them in the toolbox. I laughed when I opened it. There were quarters in the bottom, maybe a foot deep.

"What?" he said.

"I didn't know you had that many. That's why you can't get twelve to the gallon. They're too heavy."

"Maybe. But I do pay the gas stations with them. I got to count one hundred and sixty to fill it up. I see you counting in your head. That's forty dollars. But no one says nothing about it. They say they need the change."

We sat on the tailgate, and for a while we joked and swung our feet. I hadn't seen him in a week or two and we carried on better for it. But he had gotten tired of telling me how good everything was going for him. His feet hung still.

"Everything okay around here?" he asked.

"The same."

"Did you see that bumper sticker on her car?"

"Yeah."

"She's only doing that to go against me. She ain't gonna vote for it."

"I know."

"Don't ever get tangled up with a woman. Someday you might think you're ready, but they ain't like they seem at first."

He hopped down and began a slow pace from the shed to the truck, back and forth.

"I thought she was the real thing at the start," he said. "The boys at work said she was the door prize and I believed them. And it was good there for a while. You don't believe me, but it was. We ate at restaurants every night and vacationed in Fort Walton. She wore that yellow damn bikini and we bobbed up and down in the water and she whispered things in my ear like everybody on the beach was trying to listen. She'd put cool gel on my sunburn at night, and I decided right then, with her rubbing that stuff in circles across my shoulders and neck, that I was done running around."

He stopped and looked at the house.

"So we got married, and it was good until she quit noticing me. She stopped touching me under the dinner table while she talked to everyone else. That's when we still had other couple friends, before she turned them all against me. She talked all the time about taking art lessons and playing cards. She begged and begged for an exercise bike, so I got her one, and then she started going to the gym. I told myself it was all okay for a while. She'd get real friendly sometimes and soon as I'd warm up, she'd ask me to let her take dance lessons or go with the girls to play the slots in Tunica. And I'd let her 'cause I felt good. And when I stopped working at the bank with all those bankers who panted after her, that was the end. That's when she stopped noticing me at all. She says my pots are embarrassing. She doesn't yell about it. She smirks at me. Makes me batty. She talks on the phone too soft for me to hear, leaves in the vehicle I bought her, and comes back after I fall asleep. I look under her car seat one day for the atlas and find a mess of toilet paper with lipstick all over it. Now what should I make of that?"

He picked up a rock and aimed for the kiln. A branch knocked it down.

"She don't know what she's doing to me," he said. His voice had gotten away from him. "People from all over are talking about me now. Not just from Alabama. A boy I used to know called me from St. Louis. He saw me in the paper. And she don't take notice, Junior. But I take notice of her." He kicked a few times at an old, rubbery root. "I go to driving faster than hell some nights now, like I used to do. Rode the yellow line and cut my lights out coming down Chambers County last week. She don't know."

I didn't like the way he was looking at me. I swung at a wasp.

"I got to be going," he said. "Got to go clear to Evergreen for a rally in the morning. Black folks' rally but they're giving me two hundred dollars just for showing up. They're madder than hell about the tax. That's my fee now. Two hundred dollars. Cash."

He climbed in the cab. I hopped off and closed the gate. He pulled the door shut, turned the vent window in on himself, and backed out. I went inside. Robyn's cat was picking its feet up and down between Robyn's legs, its back arched and its tail flicking. Robyn was laughing into the telephone.

I went to my room and read catalogs and magazines while the radio played a station from the college in Columbus. But I couldn't take it easy like usual. I kept thinking about the icebox, kept trying to give the kid a face.

I couldn't fall asleep. So sometime after Robyn had driven off, after it was good and dark and I knew the mosquitoes had quit, I went downstairs and stole a few handfuls of cat food. I dropped them in a paint bucket and walked through the field to the pond. The night was hot and still. I tossed the food in, flipped the bucket, and took a seat.

After a few minutes the surface began to roll. The catfish poked their whiskers into the night and slurped the stuff. It was a secret of mine I had learned some years before. I used to take a can of gravel and practice my aim on their flat, shovel heads. But that night I was satisfied with the noise they made and with their murky, bulging eyes, and for a while I didn't think about nothing.

Then I remembered that for several summers there was always one fish that had a hook and bobber attached to its mouth. It had broken Gid's line during one of our old contests—the line had snapped inside the push-button reel, and Gid had tossed the thing in the weeds. Anyway, I would always look for this fish when I sat on the bucket. But that night the bobber never showed. And I sat there wondering if the thing had died or just lost his marking and become like the others.

3.

THE CLOUDS CAME IN THE AFTERNOONS LIKE USUAL, BUT IT HARDLY rained all summer. It wasn't very hot and uncomfortable. It was just dry, and everywhere, things looked a little worse than usual. The grass was the color of matches. The ponds were like puddles and the cows stood knee-deep in the middle. The crops were hunched like John Frederick. When it did rain, it would only get part of the county, and that part only for a few minutes.

Gid said it was the same story all over the state. He called almost every day to tell me about it. It wasn't anything to him if it didn't rain, but he'd make like it was. Just when his career was starting to roll, when he should've been wide-eyed and happy, the drought was another thing going wrong. You could add it to the season tickets, and his wife, and that the truck wasn't getting eleven miles a gallon and gas was on the rise. There were also too many skunks in Walker County and the Braves didn't have consistent middle relief. And there was this son of a bitch at one of the rallies that threw him off.

I fixed a sandwich while he told me about it from a pay phone in Dothan. The rally had been in a field near Loachapoka and there was a band of pickers and some pork butts smoking. It was going fine—the money was coming in and the beer was free—until a group of students showed up in protest. They brought posters and a bullhorn. A skinny professor was trying to make Gid look ignorant. He kept asking him if he knew that a yes vote would mean he, a professor and author, would pay more money to Montgomery, while Gideon Banks, a backwoods artist, and most of the people at the rally, would pay less. Gid kept telling the man that he knew all he needed to know. Some of the students started yelling and some people got pushed. The deputies jumped in quick and broke it up. The music stopped. The crowd parted then and the professor and his students left.

That night Gid was in Auburn for the season opener. He was at a tailgate with some people but he couldn't act regular. He was drinking a lot of beer but it wasn't making it better. The rally had spoiled on him and now he didn't care about the game. Then he saw the professor a few spots down, serving Brunswick stew to all of his friends. The man didn't see him though. And Gid just drank and watched.

"I kept thinking I should go frighten him a little," he told me. "But I couldn't believe he was the kind who would want to tailgate. And everyone kept coming up for his stew. It was a ten-gallon pot. It made me think that maybe he wasn't a queer, you know what I mean?"

"Yeah," I said.

"I'm not saying he weren't a son of a bitch."

"I know."

"I should've tied him up and taken his ticket."

"Did you get in?"

"I heard it on the radio. I didn't try for a ticket. It's just as well too, because it was over before half. The coaches got a boy under center who gets too confused and I don't got to tell you why. You watched it. They horsewhipped us up front and the boy just stood there and took the sacks."

"You going next week?"

"To Atlanta? I don't see the point. Georgia Tech's no good and they play on Astroturf. We'll win easy but it don't matter anymore."

He told me he was headed to Eufala. Then over by Tuscaloosa and up to Muscle Shoals. The vote was coming up and he was wanted all over. The next Saturday Auburn got beat again. It wasn't very close.

——

On the day of the vote, a Tuesday, John Frederick and I were parked outside the Green Store. An afternoon storm was blowing in. It got loud and windy, and we whispered. Then the rain came heavy for half an hour. Lightning lit up everything, and the thunder didn't wait. Then the rain turned to hail and bounced off the windshield, and when the hail stopped, the storm had moved on. Only a mist was left. I looked at the icebox. It had a wet cardboard sign that said. "No Ice," and the rain had bled the lettering. A bouquet of field flowers was twined to the handle, but the rain had put most of the petals on the gravel.

Sweet Pants pulled up with the top up on her convertible and squeezed it a few inches away from my window. I rolled with my left hand, coaxing the glass down with my right.

"Boys been to vote?" she asked. Her head was in my window.

"Can I ask you which man you boting for?" John Frederick said.

Sweet Pants laughed and rubbed some raindrops into my arm. On her hand was a wart and some peeling nail polish.

"We ain't voting for any man," she said. "We're voting against the man today. I mean, I ain't voting but everyone else is. Governor's trying to get more of our money. Says the state's broke. But hell if we ain't all broke too. I'd a voted against his ass if my ass wasn't drunk. And if I had a voting card. Government thinks I'm dead. And I'll stay a dead ass as long as I can so they can't get my money. But you boys should vote so they don't get yours."

"I neber did that. My driber's license been dead eleven years…"

"You see that hail?" she said. "I saw it knock a vulture out of a tree."

"You did?"

Her breath was yellow. It stayed with us for a while after she had driven off. The mist was getting me. I tried to roll up the window but it was stuck. I crawled to my knees to get both hands on the top of the glass. I could pull up one side a little, then the other side to match. Halfway up, the crank worked.

"We don't know where any of our money goes," John Frederick said. "They could hab it buried in their attic. You know what? We got snakes and scorpions they don't do nothing about. That's true. They need to get all these snakes and alligators out of here before more people die. That's right."

He closed his eyes.

"An old man snake is staying under my bed and I can smell him under there. He's under there and do you know a woman snake was crawling towards my door this morning and I had to shew her away. She was coming to be with the man snake. She want to twist and turn like they do and juke some babies. But I said no. No ma'am. You leave here or I'll put you in my pot. I hab a mind to burn the man snake out. But I don't want to burn my cobers too. And that old snake will leabe in the winter. Find him a warmer place. That draft will run him off."

The mist was gone. John Frederick rolled his window down and the fog shrunk on the windshield. The low red sun made the doors of the icebox glow. They beamed back at us. Beyond the building the purple sky hung like a cloak, tucked away behind the flaming treetops at the back of the field. To the north, Georgia was getting wet. Lightning cut the gray.

Horace Green's dog wandered out from under an old pew and took a drink from a puddle. He looked over his shoulder towards us, then over the other towards the highway, then walked raggedly to a wooden light pole and marked it. He saw sparrows flitting in and out of a thicket, took a step towards them, sniffed, then turned back towards the dry spot under the pew. He stopped on the way, sat on the wet, chalky gravel, and kicked at a spot behind his ear. His haunches were all dirty as he sneezed his way to the pew.

John Frederick said, "That's an animal with a home. Yeah. He's already there."

On the ride back he sang. It was story-song about a murder told by a working man with a nice family. But the refrain was the main thing. It went:

I'm the man that let him die,
Nobody knows but I.

We bumped down the long clay drive and the old man sang it hard and sharp. And as we splashed through the puddles, I wondered if he really believed that he had ever done anything wrong. He sang songs like that all the time. Songs that called himself a liar and killer. They bothered me.

He cut the motor under the pecan tree. He kept singing until a nut pinged on the roof, rolled down the windshield, and nested on the wiper blade.

"Did you see that?" He grabbed my arm. "It still summer and a pecan fall. That mean the tree is too thirsty to hold them anymore. It be so dry for so long. It rain this afternoon. But the tree don't get him a drink 'cause the rain can't get into the dry ground. It all run down to the pond and this tree is still thirsty. That nut will not be good to eat. You know when they good is when they taste like brown sugar."

I figured it would still be a few weeks before they'd be ready. Then I'd rake them, and we'd sit in lawn chairs with the nuts piled in our laps and plastic sacks tied to the chair handles. Cupping two in our palms, we would break one against the other and pull the shells away. And for a couple of Sundays John Frederick would give little bags of them to the widows at the church.

He sat there smiling. He said, "That rain will be enough for the turnips. They late coming but they got what they need now. I'll get them tomorrow. Yeah."

I got out and walked into the woods. The storm had blown some leaves from the trees and they lay bright and belly-up on the path. As I walked through the undergrowth, I lifted my arms to make myself thinner. I always did that after a rain, but it never worked. The leaves still brushed me and their raindrops sopped my shirt. Nearing the field, I remembered something. I veered off the path to a hackberry and got down on my knees. I scraped the ground off the wet, rotting leaves and found the rusty rim of a wagon wheel that circled the tree like an old hoopskirt. I ripped it free from the threaded roots and held it at my waist. When I was younger, I would imagine how the wheel ended up there. I made up stories about Indians and settlers. This time I just thought about how they were stuck with each other, the tree and the wheel. And I wondered what would free them first, the rotting or the rust.

I dropped the rim and patted the dirt from my hands. Then I sat on a rock and listened to the birds. They always sounded happier after a rain. Probably not for the rain, I thought, but because it had stopped. Night was coming but I wasn't in a hurry to get out of there like usual. In the forest, darkness doesn't fall. It rises from the ground. I watched it climb up the tree trunks, and as it did, tree frogs began to chatter and drowned out the birds. A wind slithered through the undergrowth and gave me a chill. When I hopped the fence into the tall grass, a thin scarf of red lay above the trees to the west. It faded upward to purple, then to blue where a few stars had lit. Across the field, under the trees by the shed, I saw the cab light in Gid's truck.

"Did you see them coyotes on the fence line?" he asked when I came walking up.

I nodded.

"Rare to see them together like that. Means there's less food now. Here, give me a hand with this thing. Hop up in there and hand him to me. Be easy with him."

I jumped up in the truck bed and took the governor apart. We carried him in pieces to the shed. Gid broke a splinter from the woodpile and leaned against the wall. He folded his arms and picked his teeth with the stick.

"Fella had a late crop of sweet corn," he said. "Rich fella with pretty daughters. Got it all in my teeth. Good corn though."

I climbed up on the lawn mower seat.

"You would've liked these daughters, Junior. They were a little older, but the one who was divorced was something. You should've seen the way she walked around."

"Did she have any pretty daughters?"

"No, damn it. She weren't that old. I'd say thirty."

"How old was your momma when she had you?"

"That ain't your business. But she was fifteen."

He threw his toothpick at me.

"Well ye ole tax plan went over well," he said. "The counting ain't finished, but it looks like the thing got shot down 2 to 1. Newspapers might print profanity tomorrow. They so damn mad they can't see through the tears. One newspaper editor—editor of the whole paper—said he wanted to put me in his column. I wouldn't talk to the boy though. I told him I knew his kind and I wouldn't let him hang any blame on my beak."

Gid peeled another splinter and dug in his teeth. He pulled it back and studied it. Then he spit some kernel skin. Above us some moths started haloing the lightbulb.

"I haven't told her yet but I ended up giving most of the money to the cause," he said. "I got to feeling bad about it while I was driving from place to place. Dumped it at the Montgomery headquarters last Sunday after the game. They told me it would help pay for ads on the TV. I felt good to be gone of it. I had it changed into paper and it was making me all itchy and I was having dreams I didn't like. I kept two thousand though. Expenses. Way gas has been I should have kept a little more. But we'll be fine. People know me now. I even got an invitation to the big show in Tuscaloosa next month. I didn't even have to apply. And you know those collectors from New York will buy a sack of ditch weeds if you sign your name to it."

I looked at the governor. His head sat on the floor beside the toilet, and his face had a lot of nicks. "What are you gonna do with him?" I asked.

"That boy in Columbus wants it for his museum, but I don't know if I'll let him have it. I don't like him that much."

"We could drop him in the pond for the crappie."

"There ain't no crappie in there."

"I caught two yesterday."

"You're a liar. Your old friend stole all the crappie four years ago whether you believe it or not. And the perch, and most of everything else."

"No. I caught two the size of my hand."

"We can't sink him in the pond, Junior. He's famous."

Gid grabbed his bag from the cab and handed it to me. Inside Robyn was on the sofa talking on the phone.

"I got to go," she said and clicked off.

I put Gid's bag down and stood by the kitchen counter. Robyn got up. She wore hair curlers and a bathrobe.

"Your feet. Look at your feet," she said. She was talking to me. "How many times have I told you? If you're gonna go stomping through the woods to play with your friend, that's your own business. But this floor is my business and I won't have muddy feet drug across it."

I started laughing. But I backed out the door and went around to the side steps. In the mudroom I heard her lighting into him. I untied my boots. They were wet on the toes, and some grass and burs clung to the laces. I pulled them off, plucked a seed tick from my ankle hair, flattened it with my thumbnail, and washed it down the sink. Then I lay across the washer and dryer and listened.

"I work every day, nine to five or six, and you're telling me that your four months of this brought us two thousand dollars. Give it to me."

"Wait."

"Give it to me. Two thousand dollars."

"I gave you nine hundred dollars last month."

"That was July 15. The first time you paid the mortgage in a year. You know it's bad enough to have a husband who's a carney. All those newspaper pictures are humiliating. But I have to pull the whole load too. It's making me into a man here."

"It went to the cause," Gid offered. "Made a…it made a…"

"A difference? That's sweet, but tell me you don't believe that. Nobody gave that tax two shots in hell. And when are you gonna get it through that you can't make up for your mistakes with a little charity? Is that what happened here? You finally got a lot of decent people to buy your little pots, to pay their hard-earned money for bullshit, and then you got to feeling bad about it so you gave all the money away."

"Rich people buy it mostly," he said.

"Trying to make yourself feel better's what you're doing. Just like bringing him home because you couldn't get the job done with me."

It was over like that. He never could think as fast as her. He just froze up. I knew what came next. He'd say he loved her and she'd bang through the cupboards. She liked to punctuate her victories that way. And that's how it went. I heard the front door close softly and I heard Robyn go upstairs. Gid started his truck, and there was the whine of the motor reversing fast.

After a while I went in the kitchen. I took a jar of pickles from the fridge and sat on the couch. The governor was talking on the TV, saying everything that was hard was about to get a little harder, but hell, we'll just have to pull together. He said something about civil rights, something else about family, and he tried to quote Paul Bear Bryant from memory. His wife was standing behind him in a man suit. She was plain looking and sad.

Robyn's heels were sounding through the ceiling. They hammered down the stairs. She had a no-food-on-the-couch rule, so I put the pickle jar between my feet. She came into the room and stopped behind the couch. Her perfume irritated my nose.

"Hey," she said.

I looked. She held a hundred-dollar bill.

"I'm sure he didn't pay you for the work you done around here."

I let the bill hang in her hand.

"You can have it," she said.

I changed the channel.

"Take it," she said again.

I turned the volume up.

"No?" she said casually. "Of course not, coming from me. You're loyal to him. You always have been and I don't get it. It's his fault you're like this and he don't think nothing's wrong. Here. Take it. Take the money and go get drunk. Go wave it around and get a girl to pay attention."

She waved it in my face and the end brushed my nose. Then she laughed and did it again. And she got down by my ear and scratched her nails through my hair.

"Or are you gay?" she said. "Huh? Is that it? Yeah. It makes sense now. You got a sugar daddy on the other side of the woods. An old brown daddy."

"That's right," I said. "And he asked me to marry."

She dropped the bill and left.

The governor was on a few stations. I turned him off and got up. But I knocked the pickles over. They lay there on the Oriental rug like a litter of wet rats. I kicked them under the couch and put the jar in the trash. Then I microwaved some hot dogs and cheese and dipped them in yellow mustard. After that, I took a long shower. I sat down in the bath and listened to the radio turned up loud.

There was a new girl DJ at the college station in Columbus. She was confident for a new one, and between songs she talked about the tax vote. She told people to call in. I didn't know the songs she played. But she said her name was Leddy. And I lay there under the water and remembered the girl I knew with that name. She'd wear a dirty dress and she'd let Twizzlers hang from her lips like cigarettes.

I woke up when the water turned cold. The DJ had changed. The clock on the radio said it was almost midnight. I heard someone walking downstairs—heavy boot steps—so I knew it was Gid. That was good. Robyn would have said something about the hot water. I got dressed.

Coming downstairs I smelt the pickles. It was stronger as I came into the kitchen, more vinegary and sick. I found Gid spread out on the floor. He lay there like a spilt drink, and I saw that his boots had dirtied up the linoleum. I stood over him and watched him blink.

He said flatly, "God help me, Junior."

I smelt a little whiskey and figured him drunk. I stuck a toe in his ribs. But he was limp. He had left the door open and a moth hit me on the face. I went to close it, but a noise drew me out on the porch. In the distance some dogs howled. They were mimicking a siren.

4.

I REMEMBER THE BLUE LIGHTS ARCING IN THE NIGHT. WE HUNCHED through the tall grass, towards the wall of trees, and the lights swung across the treetops. I helped Gid over the fence, and the woods were black around us. A hay weed was caught in my toes. I stopped to pull it free. Then we were walking the deer path. I remember the way the moon dropped here and there through holes in the forest ceiling. I remember the trees blacker than the night. We slipped between them, and the leaves weren't wet anymore. They had soaked it all up. I pushed through the undergrowth, and the branches whipped back at Gid.

I came out of the trees and squinted at the moonlight. John Frederick's place threw a long, narrow shadow. His car set in the shadow of the pecan tree, and the field was behind it in the silver light. Gid came out behind me. He was pale, and breathing rough.

I went up the ramp and opened the door. My feet were wet and the floor was gritty, and I walked the narrow hall to his bedroom. There was no door there, just a frame, so I stuck my head around. The old man was sitting on the end of his bed, his knees against the wall. I pulled back quick. And I thought, *I have never been here at night. In eight years, I have never seen the man after dark.* I gave a few taps on the frame.

I looked again and saw him sitting the same way, his hands on his knees and a gauzy tank top on his round shoulders. I knocked harder.

"Who did that another time?" he said. "Say your name."

I went in.

"Who has come?" he said.

I moved towards him and reached slowly for his shoulder. His eyes opened then, and before I could pull my hand back, he snatched it. He held it tight and stared at me for a while. But I couldn't think of anything to say. I didn't know why I had come there. I pulled my hand free and patted his shoulder. And I said I was sorry and turned to go.

"Oh. Okay. Yeah," he said. "I put my shoes on and my hat too, then I come with you."

Gid was leaning against the tree, his arms drawn inside his overalls, and his shoulders up by his ears, shivering. I walked down the ramp and stopped at a drooping branch. I pulled a leaf off and shredded it.

He said, "I should probably go on back, Junior."

I took another leaf.

"Or maybe your pal can give me a ride over to Sheriff Turnbo's. Sumbitch'll be happy to lock me up."

Then he took a few steps and threw up. John Frederick came down the ramp, buttoning up a shirt. Gid wiped his mouth on his sleeve. Then he walked towards the old man with his hand out. And I thought, *They have never met. They are the only two people I know, and they are strangers.* They shook hands.

"I feel good this morning," John Frederick told him. "The sun don't catch me yet. I get it going before he can."

Gid waited. "Well, me and Junior need a lift to the sheriff's office and we were hoping you might help us."

John Frederick looked proudly at his car and put his hands in his pockets. Then he stared out over the sunken field. Gid looked at me, then back at the old man.

"Sir," he said. "If you could give us a ride, we would be glad to make it up to you."

"You said you need to see Mr. Sheriff?"

Gid straightened up against the tree as John Frederick shuffled closer. He put a finger on Gid's breastbone, and said, "Did you know already that I'b been dribing with a dead driber's license for eleven years?" He measured the impression this had left.

Gid gave him a pat and started walking.

"Junior," he said, "I'm gonna start that way. If they pick me up before I get there, then good. I want to lay down in a bed."

I shook John Frederick's hand and followed after Gid. But we stopped when the car door opened. He turned it over, cut the lights off and on a few times, then swung it around the tree and pulled beside us. He opened his door and said he could let us out in front as long as he didn't have to go inside.

So we bumped down the drive. Other places, tilted things with dogs chained to the axles, lay like old hounds in the moonlight. They sat back off the drive, and their shadows yawned to the east. We turned out and headed north. John Frederick drove with his brights on, and the other cars flashed us.

"In the daytime peoples wave. In the dark they pop their lights," he said. "Rich cars can do that."

We did thirty-five in a fifty, and a Bronco passed us on a curve. We passed the Green Store, and I saw the dead flowers on the icebox and the dog under the pew. A mile later there were police lights in the middle of the highway. There were cars backed up on both sides. A few officers stood on the yellow lines and shone their flashlights in the windows.

When we had inched to the front, I turned to look at Gid. But I didn't see him. We pulled up and the officer put his light on John Frederick.

"Driver's license," the officer said.

"Oh yeah," John Frederick said. "Well I do hab one and I

wouldn't go without it. But I should tell you about it first. I got my driber's license when I got this vehicle and that was my sixty-first year. I am now seventy-four."

The officer put his light on me. I nodded.

"We got bigger things to do tonight than check licenses," he said. "You boys get on home and be safe."

"Why, I mean to thank you," John Frederick said. "Yes sir. We got to go see the sheriff, then we will."

But the officer had already walked to the car behind us. We eased on.

Gid hollered from the back. I looked over the seat and saw him on the floorboard. He was bent over the hump, struggling to get his arm over the lip of the seat. I got on my knees and grabbed the straps of his overalls. He pushed himself upright. His hat was on the floor and his head was wet. He rolled the window down and leaned into the breeze. I kept looking back but he only watched the night through the window. A few minutes passed and I saw the flagpole that marked the sheriff's office. Gid stuck his head between the front seat headrests.

"What do you say we go on a little piece?" he said. "I think I changed my mind about the police."

John Frederick was humming. The flagpole climbed higher.

"What about we go on a little ways?" Gid tried again. "Reckon a few miles would be too much trouble?"

There were several officers in the parking lot. We were going pretty slow.

"Hey ole buddy. Hey," Gid said.

We eased on by. Gid leaned back. The damp wind beat through his window and made the car pulse like a big speaker, so I cracked my window to even it. I lay my head against the glass and watched the yellow lines. For a while I imagined what Gid could have done. I had a few ideas. Each one put a knot in me. But then I did the thing I know best. I didn't think about nothing. The yellow lines slipped under the car and John Frederick sang:

What are they doing in heaven today,
Where sin and sorrow are all gone away?
Peace abounds, like the river they say,
But what are they doing there now?

The yellow lines moved to the center of the car. The old man
had closed his eyes. I pulled the wheel back and woke him up. And
for another hour we drove real easy. On the curves he'd take his foot
off the gas and the headlights would flicker. Bugs were dying on the
windshield and I watched them like a child under a mobile. I con-
sidered nothing. Maybe if I would've known that night how things
would go for us, if I could have seen it all written out in a book, I
might have taken the wheel and yanked us into a ditch. But today
I am not wishing I would have done it. John Frederick used to say
something about that. Something about not going back to Egypt.

He pulled into a church and swung around back. There was a
shed there, and Gid said that we would lay down behind it for a
while. The old man said he would wait in the car. I took a blanket
from the trunk and spread it against the shed. I got down on it but
Gid went to a fence and bowed his head. Then, when he finally
joined me, he left his shoes on. He told me to lay back and sleep.

"Will you be able to?" I said.

"I got to figure some things."

"You want any help?"

"No I don't."

A granddaddy longleg walked across the blanket. I let him crawl
up on my arm for a minute. Then I took his leg and threw him. The
churchyard was freshly cut. I looked across the top of the grass and
saw the spider climbing across it.

"The Braves won tonight," I said.

Gid sat up against the shed. "Go to sleep, Junior."

"They came back from three down in the eighth."

"But they were playing the Brewers."

The spider was coming back. He was very slow.

"Who won the All-Star game this year?" I said. "I can't remember."

He didn't answer. I threw the spider again. One of his legs stuck on my finger. I tried to see how far I could stick it up my nose before I sneezed. Then I wiped my eyes and rolled over. Gid's knees were drawn against him and he was dark in a shadow that had crept from the shed. He twitched a little, but I couldn't tell if he was sleeping.

I dreamed of a field without fences. A peanut field. John Frederick was sitting in a row with his hat off, eating nuts. There was a carton of milk between his legs and the skin from the nuts hung on his beard. A child was walking up the row, a long way off. When he got closer, it was Gid. He was a midget and he held a paper lunch bag. He stood behind the old man and the old man went on eating. Gid took a handful of cotton from the bag and dropped it on him. He kept taking handfuls out of the sack and dropping them on the old man until the cotton piled over his legs and climbed his chest and, finally, buried him. Then Gid waddled off. A breeze came then and scattered the cotton. And only the milk was there. I turned to walk away. But I tripped on the old man. He was sitting behind me, doing the same as before.

IN THE MORNING THE DEW WAS ON US. IT WAS JUST COMING LIGHT, AND I shook Gid. He sat up fast, jerking his head around and cursing himself. I pulled my arms under my chest and put my face in the blanket. I thought I could sleep a little longer while he figured something. But the old man started talking on the other side of the shed. We listened for another voice but it was only him.

He started the car when we got in and let it run for a minute.

"Maybe you could take us north a little ways," Gid said. "Up by Opelika."

"Oh yeah."

"It's not too far."

"I went to Opelika in 1989 with my baby's sister. She hab a boyfriend there that she want me to see. And I saw him and said he was fine to marry."

"Well maybe you can visit them this morning."

"They neber did marry. He found out about another woman."

"Make a right out of here," Gid said. "I know where we are."

We found the main road and went north. The sun came soft and colored the clouds at the other end of the sky. The newspaper bags were wet in the yards and the porch lights were still on, and I thought of everybody laying in their beds or standing at their coffeepots. In the fields the calves followed their mothers.

I lay my head on the window and waited for a siren. There would be a quick scene followed by some long, empty days. And after everything settled down I could get things back to normal. I knew John Frederick would let me stay with him. Maybe even build a little place in the woods behind his trailer. It would be about the same as before, but with Gid in the prison. That got me feeling bad. But then he started talking and I didn't think I would mind much if he wasn't around. Sometimes I only liked part of him.

"Does this thing go any faster, Junior?"

I didn't answer.

"How are we on gas?" he asked.

We drove slowly and Gid said something else about it. He was leaning up from the backseat. I told him it didn't make any difference.

The old man waved to the trucks we passed. He'd put his hand up, and when they had gone by, he'd jerk and watch them in the rearview mirror. I saw a sign that said we were twelve miles from Opelika.

"I got a plan, Junior."

"Good."

"I don't know how it all will go but I have an idea about starting everything new somewhere."

"In Opelika?"

"Not in Opelika."

"All right, where?"

"I know where. But it's better we don't talk about it in case the police interrogate you."

I put my feet up on the dash.

"I'll get up with you when everything settles down," he said. "It might be a little while, but I will."

"Tell me your idea. I'll tell you if it will work."

"It's a good plan; I thought of it all night, but I can't say."

"That wasn't me that told Robyn about your motorcycle," I said.

"I know it weren't you. And I shouldn't have accused you. But this ain't the same."

"It was your cousin," I said. "It was him that told."

"Damn, I know it was. But this ain't about trust. I'll check in with you when I can."

That's how he is, I thought. He doesn't know where he's going but he wants to keep it a secret. He pretends he has things he doesn't, he thinks he's a kind of man that he's not, and he gets worked up thinking those things he doesn't have, those things he's not, are starting to get away from him. He is a like a neutered bitch dog playing mother with a stuffed animal.

"There is an alligator named Stuart Big Henry that ate two children and a dog in 1963," John Frederick said. "They shot him in the side six times and got the collar out of his belly."

"All right," Gid said. "Junior, you know what I'm saying. I can get a new thing going."

"Clean break," I said.

"Okay, Junior. You tell me what you think I should do."

"Stuart Big Henry hab a bullet in his head when they got him out. It was in there since 1958."

"What are you talking about?" Gid said.

The car bucked. We pulled onto the grass. Smoke crawled out of the hood like ghosts. We got out and Gid lifted the hood with the blanket. The smoke poured out and choked him and the hood slammed shut.

"Won't it stay up by herself?" he said.

"You need to hab a stick to put in her mouth. I juke a broom handle in there," John Frederick said. He looked like he would laugh.

"Been having trouble?" Gid asked.

"I dribe her good and I don't go too fast."

"I can't have a look at her with the hood down," Gid said. "No way I can do that."

"I never dribed her too fast or too far, but she's blowed up now. Yeah. First one I eber had."

He walked around to the backseat and got a box of seeds off the floor. He poured some in his hand and put them in his pocket. They fell through his pant leg and scattered in the grass. The smoke was the unnatural kind. It was making me sick. Gid looked up and down the highway.

"Old man, someone will come and help you," he said. "Junior, tell the police you were out looking for me since last night."

He shook my hand. I said, "All right." Then he went to a wooden fence and climbed over. I watched him going through the field for the trees. His ponytail hung out from his hat and swung around. He wasn't a short man, but he walked squatty. It made me think of the time I imitated him out by the shed. He had told me that he was one-eighth Indian, and I could go to the library anytime I wanted and see pictures of real Indians walking the same way. I watched him going, and I missed him some.

But John Frederick started after him, carrying his blanket. Down the fence a little ways was a cattle guard. I followed the old man across it and we walked after Gid. He was making a wide loop around the cows. I followed the old man right through them. They had tags on their ears and they made noises. Gid walked into the woods and came to a fence. We crunched in after him.

"The hell you doing?" he said.

He put his hands on his knees.

"What are you doing?" he said again. He was breathing hard.

The cows had followed us. They were coming towards the trees.

"Where are your shoes?" Gid said.

John Frederick was looking back across the field, past the cows to his car. It was smoking more than before. Then fire came out of the hood and through the window like some NASCAR burning in the infield. Some cars cautioned past.

The cows were in the trees. They were coming and breathing

and Gid threw some sticks and hit one in the face. They came closer. But one of them smelt the fire and the rest followed her back across the field to see about it.

"Old man, go on back now," Gid said. "Go stand by it and someone will take you home."

He started walking along the fence. Again John Frederick followed. Gid looked over his shoulder as we went. But we stayed with him.

"Go on back," he said. "Damn. Just get off me and leave me to myself and let me be. If you like me, you'll do it."

We followed the fence until we came to a corner. The thing was metal there and Gid tried to climb it quick. But it was too shaky for him. After a try or two he looked up through the trees, for God maybe. And he yelled.

I got a hold of the bottom wire and bent it up so we could crawl under. Gid went first. Then I went and helped the old man from the other side.

There was no fence to follow then. I took the blanket from the old man. We went through the woods and for a while I watched hard for snakes. But it was early to be sweating that much, the blanket was heavy across my neck, and I stopped worrying about them.

Anyway, the walking was flat and the wood was old and clear underneath. John Frederick was humming most of the time. He could get pretty loud, and then it would be a groan. And he'd slip a word in there, a *baby* or a *Jesus*, and I'd laugh at him. But it was irritating Gid. He asked him if he could shut up.

6.

AFTER A WHILE WE WEREN'T MAKING IT AS FAST. WE SPREAD THE BLANKET and sat down to rest. Gid found a stick and reached in his pocket for his knife. But it wasn't there, and he decided it had fallen out when we crawled under the fence. I gave him mine and he whittled a while. A wind helped John Frederick to sleep. It cooled my sweat and took the itch away.

"What about that Atlanta bus that goes to Shorter?" Gid said. "Does that stop in Opelika?"

I shrugged.

"You got any money if it does?"

"Robyn gave me a hundred."

"I gave her that money, remember. But we might take that bus to the tracks. Maybe I could bet on the dogs and get lucky."

"Maybe we could buy a jug of water."

"I know."

"How far do you think we are?" I said.

"To the bus? Six, seven miles."

We lay back and napped. When we got up, it was afternoon and hot. Still, I had slept hard and it felt like morning again. We moved pretty quick. We crossed some clay roads and kept north. Sometimes we would hear the highway and sometimes it would be too far away. It was nicer when it was quiet, and I messed with an idea of living in the woods, us three. It was a thing I had imagined when I was younger, and I used to go around with a book of wild edible plants and berries. But after a few weeks of searching I found that nothing good grows on its own in Alabama.

We came close to the highway again and spied a gas station. We stood in the woods and checked it out. John Frederick said he would go in there and use the bathroom. So we gave him some money and asked him to get us some things. He shuffled across the highway, tipped his hat to a lady at one of the pumps, and went in.

"If he didn't have all that money, I'd say we leave him," Gid said. "He's gonna slow us down."

"He's the one that followed you," I said.

"Followed where?"

"When the car blew up and you walked off, he started after you."

"Why would he do that?"

John Frederick came out, turned a circle, and waved to the building.

"He forgot the water," Gid said.

"Maybe it's in the bag."

"No. He forgot it."

He misjudged where he had left us and entered the woods a long ways down. We went to him.

"The woman said the bathroom's broke," he said. "But I told her she was working well. Yeah."

He handed us a paper sack. The change was in there on top of some sausage biscuits, so I took the money and went for some water. The tile was cool after the pavement. I got a gallon jug. While I was waiting to pay, a man came out of the rest room. He looked at my feet and stood beside me like he would go first. I cut him off.

"That was your friend that came in here," the woman said.

I gave her the money.

"I broke a hundred for him," she said. "I usually don't do that.

If it's a fake, then we'll find him. I took his address down."

When I got back, the grease from the biscuits had wet the sides of the bag. The biscuits were the square kind that fall apart at the corners and the sausage was spicy. The whole thing had taken on the character of the heat lamp, and I ate mine happily.

We passed the jug. Gid took some matches from his pocket and tried to light the wax paper.

"I know this place," he said. "We ain't as far as I thought."

"As far from what?" I said.

"We're close to the freeway. A couple miles."

We didn't make it there before dark. There were more houses and too many nervous dogs, and we made big loops getting around them. So we stopped at dusk in a small wood and spread the blanket. Sitting there, with the air like wool and the ground hard underneath, I tried to imagine what it was like to lie in a bed with an air conditioner blowing on my feet. I scooted around until the mounds in the earth suited the shape of my back.

"Feels like we've been out here a long time," I said.

No one said anything.

"Feels like we've been walking all summer and sleeping out here the whole time with the mosquitoes." I said. "Y'all asleep? Listen to them tree frogs going. Listen to them talking over top each other as fast as they can. If you don't try to listen, it's only one clean noise. Same as if you let your eyes go blurry when you're looking at the woods. You can't pick one out. See if you can hear one frog and point to where you think he's sitting. You can hear the high-sounding ones better. The younger ones sound higher, I think."

"They hab poison in them," John Frederick said. "That's why nobody hunts them. But when they grow up and come down the trees and go to lib in the swamp, then they okay."

"Aren't the mosquitoes getting y'all?" Gid asked.

"Nooo. They neber hab. Bees like me but not the others."

"Lucky."

"That's right."

"How're your feet holding up, Junior?"

"Mosquitoes are getting them."

"I hope it don't rain," he said.

"No sir," John Frederick said. "It's not ready to do that."

He went to snoring soon. It seemed in chorus with the woods, the same short noises, just older and deeper.

My back was wet against the blanket. I sat up.

"You asleep, Junior?"

"No."

"You think they know where we are? You think someone's seen us and called?"

"Maybe they have."

"Well, it won't be bad for you if they find us. You won't be in trouble. I'll say I forced you to come along."

"Okay."

"You can find good work. Finish school. Anything you want."

"Let's not get caught," I said.

"All right. But are you falling asleep?"

I didn't answer. But I lay awake a long time. It wasn't the future that had me racing. I knew it would be fine after Gid was arrested. I'd just settle down with the old man and do as we did before. But the fleeing had me feeling like a child, running from some grownup you don't know too well, a grown cousin maybe, who is coming to tickle. I hate feeling like a kid. I half-wished that Gid would just turn himself in.

Some stars shone through the lattice of leaves. It wasn't gonna rain. Gid jolted from his sleep, snapped up like a mousetrap. He waited for his breath to settle, then lay back down. I'd been watching some bats darting insane. But then the silhouette of an owl swept blackly through the branches, and they were gone.

7.

THE SUN PEERED THROUGH THE LEAVES AND THE MORNING CAME HOT. We kept north in a tanglewood and the air itself seemed itchy. Sweat guttered salty on my lips. I kept licking it.

John Frederick kept his distance from Gid, and I hung in back. Crossing a creek I saw the hoofprints of a deer and a fawn. I stood in the water for a minute and burrowed my toes in the mud. But there was something sharp down there.

Gid pointed at a vine.

"Is that poison ivy?" he said.

"No."

"Poison oak?"

"It's not."

"Well it's poison something," he said, and strutted out ahead.

My foot didn't sting much, but watching the blood delta through my toes, I forgot my thirst for a while. Then, when my mouth was all cotton again, I asked Gid if he would carry the blanket for a while. He stopped. I held it out.

"Your foot's bloody," he said.

John Frederick looked at it and smiled.

"You want to carry it?" I said again.

"You can tote it, Junior. I don't want you to catch cold."

It was slow walking. When we made it to the freeway, we stayed in the woods and turned towards Georgia. The cars made us seem slower. I picked up a concrete rock and chucked it at a billboard pole. It was loud as a siren, and Gid nearly fell out. He saw me smiling, and he told me I could go to hell. It took him a minute to get his legs back. Then a horsefly started messing with him. It made him crazy and he blamed me for not killing the thing.

He caught it finally but he kept up the mutter. He kept saying that he would eat one good meal and then turn himself in. He would eat for an hour and taste every bite because he would never eat so well again.

"I got that boy between the eyes," he was saying. "I put it there on his forehead and I saw him looking at me. His eyes. And that's what you get for fooling with another man's wife. You get a silver bullet and you sleep for a long time. It says it in the Old Testament. And now I'll go to the prison and take a cold shower to get all this itch off me and if anyone looks at me in there, I'll go nuts, I'll be insane with the drool swinging and my eyes rolled back in my brain, and that will keep them off me."

John Frederick picked up a plastic bottle. Gid asked him if he had a problem with litter. He stooped for a paper cup and offered it to him. But the old man walked on by.

"That might be a piss jar, old man," Gid said, and he caught up with him. "That's what people do. Especially with a wide mouth like that. It's a pilgrim's john. That's what you got in your hand. Septic."

But John Frederick didn't seem to hear. He led the way, hunched like some day lily in the afternoon, and we followed slowly behind. We came to an exit. The woods ended. But before we came out of the trees, Gid handed me the pocketknife.

"Chop it, Junior," he said, and he choked his ponytail tight.

I sawed the thing and tossed it. As we aimed for the Cracker Barrel, I turned my head from the cars that passed. They blew a hot wind. Then a police car came screaming from behind. And even as my hair stood up, I knew it would be better after it was over. But the lights went on by.

John Frederick veered towards an Amoco. We stopped and watched. He went past the pumps to the store. The doors slid open but he didn't go in. He just dropped the bottle he'd been carrying in the can and came back. Gid told me to go get some shoes. He pointed me to the Wal-Mart and said that he would take the old man and get us a table. We parted. The tar was sticking to my feet so I moved to the grass. The grass was brown and sharp. It clawed my cut. I jogged across the parking lot and into the air-conditioning. I grabbed a pair of gray Velcroes for twelve bucks.

It was quick coming back. I walked a long drive that wrapped around the back of the restaurant. The shoes were nice. Maybe it was them, or maybe I just knew that in a few minutes I would have all the water I wanted, but I got to feeling pretty high. Around front, Gid and John Frederick were standing at the other end of the long porch. Music played on the speakers, and the place was busy. I took it easy through the crowd. A granddad was playing checkers with his grandson. The checkered rug was draped on a wooden barrel and the grandson was frustrated for having played into traps. He pushed his fingers in his cheeks. On the swing, a grandmother sat with her granddaughter and rocked. And the girl was told not to rock too fast. I walked past girlfriends and boyfriends holding hands, and young mothers smoking cigarettes, and truck drivers reading newspapers, and an old guy sleeping off a meal while his wife shopped in the general store, probably. A boy tried to climb the porch post. And another left his jacks on the concrete and bounced his ball to the porch ceiling. Gid and John Frederick were past the row of newspaper boxes on the short side of the door. I checked out the prices: Opelika-Auburn, Phenix City, Columbus—35 cents. Montgomery, Birmingham—50. Atlanta—75. New York—a buck. And I liked that you had to pay more if you didn't want to read about home.

"Junior," Gid said. "How do you like your shoes?"

"Velcro," I said.

He shook his head, and we stood there sweating under a broken fan. Now and then the music would hush and a woman's voice would call out a party and some rockers would rock empty. A few opened up together. Me and Gid took a couple, but the old man said he could stand.

Gid leaned into the arm of his chair and whispered.

"I seen a newspaper a boy was reading said something about the thing I done. You noticed anybody staring at me?"

"You are a little famous," I said.

"I'm serious. And you have a point. I've been traveling all over. I shook more hands than a politician. Good people too, most of them. But you can't tell who would want to turn me in. They may have a reward out on me. Posters and all. I ain't saying that everybody knows me, but some do."

"I thought you were going to turn it in?"

"I didn't say that. I said I'd think it over over some breakfast. You smell that ham?"

"Yeah."

"I never said I would turn myself in. You watch and make sure no one's watching us."

"Are you thinking of a disguise?" I asked.

He stared at the ground for a minute.

"Them are fine shoes you picked," he said.

"Thank you."

"A pair like that says you're going places."

"I like it out here on this porch."

"How much were they?"

"Eleven something."

"I came down here so you wouldn't get nervous. I know how you get in a crowd."

"I don't mind," I said. "I don't mind it."

A little girl, maybe four or five, walked up to John Frederick. She stood with her knees locked under her dress, and she held her head back and looked up at him. He was embarrassed. His shoulders bounced. The girl reached her hands for one of his. He gave it, and she set the big thing on top of her head.

"Damn," Gid said.

The girl's mother came and got her quick. She sat her down and whispered something. But the girl kept her eyes on John Frederick.

The music stopped and the speakers called, "Jameson, party of three."

"That's us," Gid said. "I gave a bluff name."

The country store was full of folks. They were looking at all the junk: the murder mysteries on tape, the grandma's paddles, the mind teasers, and the rock candy. I always thought they would do better to clean all that stuff out and add a lot of tables. Anyway, we squeezed through everybody and were shown a table next to a picture of an old Coke model in a one-piece bathing suit.

Our waitress had a lot of yellow hair piled on top of her head and the makings of a mustache. Her apron had four gold stars stiched below her name, Barbara. The stars meant she had made a career at the Cracker Barrel and could tell you the contents of the Country Boy Breakfast while she wrote your drink order and blew a bubble. The stars also meant that she didn't have to apologize for anything. Gid ordered for the two of us—eggs in a basket, sloppy, with some sausage gravy and grape jelly for the biscuits. John Frederick had a harder time. He just asked for some vegetables, and the woman, busy checking her appearance in the mule's yoke mirror, waited for him to specify. Finally she smacked the menu with her pen and said, "Them are the ones you can choose." He asked her to pick for him and said, "But I don't need any that you don't hab a pot of already."

The biscuits came quick. Gid flipped the napkin back and the steam plumed.

"I love it," he said.

I went and washed my hands. The water ran brown from them.

I soaped them twice. In the mirror I saw my face with the dried sweat and dirt. It looked like Robyn's after she had been crying. I washed it and drank some water from my hands.

Gid was fixing another biscuit when I came back. He had put one on my plate.

"She likes to talk all day," John Frederick was telling him. "She can wake up in the morning and start telling me one thing and in the night she can be telling me about the same thing. Everyone she sees she tell me if he a good one or a bad one and she always knows. But you know when she's feeling bad about it? You know she's feeling bad about it when she don't speak all day."

Gid had a mouthful. He said, "Yeah old man. And where is she now?"

John Frederick leaned far over the table. "That's what I still can't tell. One day she go to the plant and she don't come back. And that be a long time ago. I asked her sister and she say she don't know. And I think maybe somebody stole her. Or maybe someone poison her milk. I still can't tell. And I hab many ladies say to me, 'John Frederick, it's time you hab another baby in your arms,' but I say, 'No ma'am. I won't make an adulterer of you or me. No sir.'"

Gid pulled a plastic golf tee from the triangle game and traced the grains in the table. Barbara showed up with another young waitress. They put the spread on the table and Gid didn't snatch his fork as fast as usual. The old man thanked the women and started into grace. Gid nudged me and pointed at the old man's plate. It had carrots, green beans, corn, and macaroni and cheese. And he smiled a little. He always said that we were lucky to live in the only part of the world where macaroni and cheese was a vegetable.

8.

THAT NIGHT WE BEDDED UP BEHIND THE SUPER-CENTER AMONG THE kudzu. I slept hard until the trucks started unloading. Then we wandered out and started north instead of trying to make our way in the trees. Gid wanted to stroll. He said a black ant hadn't left him alone all night, and he didn't want to push through thorns anymore. He showed me his arm where the thing had bit him. It was scabbed up and down. He said they would haul him in shortly, and he'd rather walk out in the open one more time instead of knocking around the woods.

We passed a community college where Gid said all the girls who party too much at Auburn get sent. He said that place would give a girl a B just for wearing shorts, and it had almost been enough to make him try for a degree ten years ago. The bank had told him that he had gone as far as he could with a G.E.D., company policy. So he had sat on it, sat and figured and watched his wife get promoted ahead of him, and finally, decided he was an artist.

He put his hand on John Frederick's neck.

"What about you, sir," Gid said. "You want to go back to school? It's never too late."

"I won't fall out."

"It's hot," I said. "How 'bout we find some water."

"You feeling bad, old man?"

"No, sir. I was born in 1929."

"1929. And when were you born, Junior?"

"In the morning."

"You were born in 1984. You're too young to be whining about the heat. Consider your friend here. Your teacher. 1984. I was dating a girl at the bank who had a butt like two little puppies fighting in a grocery sack."

"Look at them cows," I said. "You ever seen them with a stripe like that?"

"You've seen pictures, Junior. She had that hair. She'd come walking out of the safe like she was in a music video."

"They look like Oreos."

"But I should have known. I should have got a girl my age," he said.

"You whine too much."

We wandered into a gas station for lunch. There was a big fan in there. We stood in front of it for a long time, then got hot dogs and a table by the window. Gid and John Frederick fell asleep. Business was slow and the man behind the counter felt like talking.

"Where you walking from?" he said.

I pointed south. He ran his fingers across a forehead crease and waited. I stared back and chewed my lip. He let his breath out in a whistle and picked up a newspaper. I went to looking out the window at some chicken trucks going by, feathers blowing through the wire, until the guy slapped the paper with the back of his hand.

"You see this, son?"

He was holding the paper up.

"It's a tremendously bad place we're living in. Pitchers like this every day. Some Arab blowed themselves up and got eight Jews. And seven of 'em's childrens. It's gotten so bad I can't hardly stand it. Fella can't believe his family's safe in times like this. All that happened at New York with those planes and we're letting more criminals move in every day."

He looked out the window at a man using the pay phone.

"I got a mess of Mexicans living right beside me. They's all crammed together, living like pigs with mud in their toes. And my grandkids got to sit by 'em in school. Can't learn a thing because the lady's got to spend all day teaching the Mexicans how to talk. And these kids ain't sure who their dads are. And their dads are out riding around drunk with no licenses, and the ones who ain't drunk are taking all the decent jobs. And you think the government cares?"

I nodded. The guy outside hung up the pay phone and came in. He tried to say something. But the man kept on:

"You know what I mean young fella. You're the one who should be the most worried about it. I had a lot of good years before all this started. All my people had good jobs and the country was ours for the taking. We'd ride around and raise a little hell, but it was only ever fun. Harmless kid stuff. And sure there was all that fuss in Birmingham and Selma, but I never had a problem with the blacks. They minded their business and we minded ours too. We'd raise a little hell with them but it was only for fun and no one ever got hurt. And I still ain't got a problem with them. But the Mexicans are the ones who got no pride. They work for almost free because they don't mind living like swine do. But like I said, I had a lot of good years before this place got spoiled." His lips were bubbling.

"Times are tremendously different now. For the worse too. And a kid like you has got to take the blow. The way I see it, by the time you have a family, your kids will be the minorities and they'll come home talking about how bad things are at school. Just think about that for a minute. And the parents can't vote but their childrens can. Just wait till we have one in Montgomery running the show. They'll get all the street signs changed like in Miami and your kids will think they're living in Mexico. And the streets will be full of drunks—fifteen in a van full of dope smoke. And if I was you, I wouldn't marry no blond woman unless you mean to put a pistol in her purse."

The customer put his hands on the counter.

"Yessir. What'll it be?" the man said, but he didn't wait for the boy to answer. He turned it back to me.

"You're familiar with the governor's tax referendum?" he said. "I'm sure you are. I'll tell you that he only had to do one thing to get that sucker passed. Just say I got a third of the new money earmarked for bus tickets for all of these Mexicans that are taking your jobs. We'll send them all home and your kids can learn again in school. You know what 'earmarked' means, don't you? I know you do. You're a smart one."

"I'll take a pack of Lucky's," the customer said. "Lights, if you got them."

"We don't got Lucky's."

The guy looked out the window and pointed to a Lucky sign hanging from the porch rafter. He said something about false advertising, that he didn't even smoke anymore, just that he was back in the county visiting his folks for the first time in a long while and the sign had reminded him of high school. The story didn't do much for the man. He looked at me, then back at the customer, who was already moving for the door.

"I'm sorry to bother you," he said. "But one more thing. Do you know how far I got to go to get cell phone service?"

After he had driven away, the man said I looked like I could use another dog.

"Sure," I said.

He brought me one. I squirted mustard down the pink meat.

"You won't be one of those that moves away and leaves their home," he said.

"No sir."

"Your boys are pretty tuckered."

Gid opened his eyes. The sun was in them. He hid them with his hand.

"I seen you walking up from a long way off," the man said. "And that's the way it is now days. People are afraid to give people a lift anymore. And it's a shame, but you can't blame them really. Where did you say you was headed?"

"Just up a little ways. Got a friend in Lafayette," Gid said. "Slide out Junior. My leg's asleep."

"It's more than a little ways to Lafayette," the man said. "About eight and a quarter. Who's your friend?"

"Oh. It's really my cousin. Boy named Dobson. Bennett Dobson."

"Bennett Dobson? Can't say I know him and that's funny."

"He's a newcomer," Gid said. "Just came in recently. Had a bad divorce and wanted to make a fresh go of it. He drives a beer truck out of Opelika. Day runs in Lee County. But he likes living up here. It's further from his old girl and pretty up this way."

The man went back to the counter and wrote something down.

"Dobson Bennett," he said.

"Yeah," Gid said. "Wake up your friend, Junior. We need to walk on."

I leaned across and touched John Frederick's arm. He blinked for about a minute. Then he got off his seat and held one finger up by his face. And he sang:

Two little boys, lying in the bed.
One rolled over and the other one said,
My momma make shortnen' bread,
My momma make shortnen' bread.

I laughed at him and he laughed back.

"That's a song my momma sang. Shortnen' bread was what I needed, and she neber need a doctor to tell her."

"C'mon old man," Gid said.

"Let me give you a ride up to Mr. Dobson Bennett's," the man said. "I'll lock the store down for half an hour. We'll go in my truck."

"No. We'll walk. We'd rather," Gid said.

"No you won't either. Not up a highway full a drunks," he said, and held the wooden door for us.

I sat in the corner of the bed with my arms stretched on the ledges and my head against the cab window. The wind put my hair in my eyes and beat my arm hair like mats of field grass. I saw a hawk on a wire and wondered if it was sleeping like that. I wished the guy had let me nap. The road rolled and bounced away from me like toilet paper. I saw a sign that said we were 43 miles from home and 202 from the ocean, as we headed further and further away from the two things that had always seemed similar and strange to me. The road widened to four lanes and there were white houses behind long yards of groomed grass. The yards were shaded by old trees that wore tire swings like jewelry. Then we came into town. And the buildings were one story with simple signs. We stopped at the light and some men eating ice cream on a bench acknowledged our driver in the way old men do. Then we passed the courthouse and eased into a corner gas station.

Gid got out and hurried into the store. He came out with the bathroom key, fiddling with his overall hooks as he went around to the side door. I hopped down.

"I hope it weren't the dogs," the man said. "I only put them in the water this morning."

We stood in the sun by the truck. Gid was in there for a long time.

"I'm sorry," the man said. "I'm Connie Bivens."

He held his hand out.

"Merit," I said.

"John Frederick Templeton White. Yeah."

"How do y'all know each other?"

"He came walking out of my woods when I was sixty-six," John Frederick said.

"All right. Well. Your pop said he would call his cousin from the pay phone. I better go on back and open up shop before the chicken houses let out."

We shook his hand again.

"You're a quiet one," he said. "But remember what I told you."

Gid came out as soon as he had driven off. He dropped the key inside.

"I don't care for him," he said. "He kept saying he had met me somewhere. But I can't remember. He may be a queer."

We stood there by the air hose. I lifted my foot to see if my soles were melting.

"I'm gonna find us a soft place to sleep tonight," he said. "There's a woman who lives up here who I met with the governor."

"Is she married?" I asked.

"She's a nice person. She's got a fruit stand."

I doubted he really knew the place. But it was there, north of town, just off the road under a pair of old trees. John Frederick shuffled up to a table of summer squash and let out a little howl. A dog lifted his mouth from the dust and looked at him. Then the woman was in the doorway and the old man took his hat off. Gid started towards her.

"I was just coming through and didn't want to pass by without checking in," he said.

She just looked at him, at us. She had no upper lip and no chin. And she wore Carhartt coveralls with cement stains. They were rolled a lot at the bottom, and they made her seem even shorter than she was. She went back inside for a minute and came out with a bag of stuff. It was full of fruit and tomatoes, and she handed it to Gid. He leaned forward under the weight of it. She nodded at me. I put my hands in my pockets. She looked at John Frederick, then back at Gid. Birds fought in the trees, cars passed, and sweat ran down the back of my legs. The dog lifted his head to watch the birds but grew bored with them and lay his mouth back in the dust.

"I thought we would have a little rain," she said finally. Her voice didn't match her. It was windy.

"How's business?" Gid asked.

"Just the same."

I was looking at the ground but I could see John Frederick shuffling from table to table, his hands folded behind him.

"Good and dirty," she said.

"But we smell good," Gid said. "Like I said, I didn't want to pass through without checking in."

"I guess I could close up early."

"You don't need to do that."

But she was already back inside. Gid handed me the bag and made a try for a wink.

———

Her name was JoBell Bunting. It said so on her welcome mat. She made scrambled eggs for supper with bacon and sliced tomatoes. She gave us each a glass of orange juice and a can of Budweiser. We ate quietly. She wasn't the kind that talked to fill space. For dessert we had bread and jelly. While she was folding a slice, she said, "I seen the papers," and she looked at Gid.

He curled up a little, like one of her hands had him by the neck. And he rocked back and forth, but barely, the way a reed will move in still water. She got up and ran the faucet in the skillet. She took an apple from the windowsill and said, "I'll be back later. Don't go nowhere."

Then she put some quilts and towels on the couch. After the screen door had clapped shut, Gid went to the sofa.

"She won't tell," he said.

I went out on the porch and stared after the heels of her truck. I stayed out there a long time. I drank a beer on the steps and watched a mule eating grass. I got a couple more cans and watched a low, penny-colored moon rise and whiten. I got very tired, but it was nice to know that I could go inside whenever I wanted. The night wind played with a little sugar maple. The leaves were silver underneath, and I imagined a great fish reflecting the sun.

I went in. Gid and John Frederick were asleep on the couches. On the carpet were smeared white footprints. They led from the bathroom to the old man. I rubbed one with my hand and smelt it. He had filled his socks with baby powder.

I took a warm shower and put my clothes back on. I found a place on the carpet beneath the air conditioner and pulled a quilt over my head.

"You awake, Junior?" Gid said sometime later.

"Yeah."

"I think I slept better in the woods."

"Did she ever come home?" I asked.

"A little while ago. She don't sleep much."

"Where was she?"

"Bricking a chimney somewhere."

I pulled the blanket off my head.

"I ain't lying," he said. "That's her other job. Makes me tired to think about it."

"At night?" I said.

"Yeah. She's a worker."

9.

GID WAS MAKING A LOT OF NOISE WITH THE CABINETS. SINCE THE DAY HE brought me to live with him he couldn't stand for me to sleep while he was about. He brought me coffee the first morning. I may have been ten. And he set it on the table, over and over, until I opened my eyes. Lately he'd learned to just turn off my ceiling fan, "So you don't dry out." I don't think Robyn was right. Gid didn't bring me around because he really thought I would fix their problems, that I could make everything feel like a home. Even he couldn't have believed that a presence like mine would be any kind of balm. I think he just wanted me around for some company at the bottom, or maybe a bottom to stand on.

We sat and ate. John Frederick was outside somewhere and Gid wanted to know why he had put that powder in his socks. Why he had to embarrass us like that.

I saw my name on a note across the table. It said, *Hang around here today. Tell Merit he can walk down to the stand if he wants.*

I folded it a bunch of times.

"Don't do that," Gid said.

I opened it and set a banana on top.

"You gonna go down there?" he asked.

I shrugged.

"She's not as rough as she comes off. And she likes you for some reason."

I found John Frederick on the porch. I sat beside him and rocked and the shadow of the roof fell across our feet. Now and then his chair would stop and he would be dozing. I liked to look at him while he slept. His face didn't hang so much, like he slept without memory.

In the meadow some guys were walking after a truck, tossing the hay on the trailer. And beyond the meadow, under the trees, was the fruit stand. I rolled my pants up, went down the steps, and headed for it. But halfway there I came on back.

She rode back soon for lunch. We had tomato sandwiches on toasted bread. I dipped my chips in the mayonnaise that dripped on the plate. But I couldn't enjoy it because Gid would hardly eat. He folded his plate and stood up.

"It's time we move on, Miss," he said. "It was nice of you to take care of us and I want to make it up to you when I'm able."

"Where you gonna go?"

"Just up the way a bit. I got some other friends to pay a visit to."

"Then I'll give you a lift," she said.

He took his coffee to the window.

"Just stay here," she said. "Till you think of something."

He went outside. The screen door slammed behind him. JoBell put our plates in the trash, then went after him. I stretched out on the couch. I could hear their voices on the porch, but not what they were saying. She came in and nodded at me, then went to her room and closed the door.

———

When Gid woke me up it was time for supper. We ate a rotisserie chicken she had picked up from the grocery. She really couldn't cook much. Gid was fine. In the middle of the table was a pitcher of Queen Anne's lace. He told me later that he had cut it on the fencerow.

"Do you remember that man who kept wanting to kiss the governor?" he asked her.

"I remember."

"Was he right?" he said.

She shook her head. "He's a simple one."

"Nobody told me," Gid said. "I didn't know what to make of him."

"What did you do with that statue?" she asked.

"It's in the shed."

"I would buy it from you."

"What do you want with him? I mean, you could have him if you want, but I don't know what for."

"I think it's handsome, and it made me smile. I could put him out on the porch for company."

"You might have to fight this one for him. He thought we could drop him in the pond for the fish. But dry as it's been I think his ears would stick out."

"It's not a bad idea at all. But he would be better on my porch. How much would get him from you?"

"Not too much," he said. "I owe you anyway."

"Maybe we could work out a trade."

"Tell that one you told me about that mule you traded for a microwave."

"It was fifty dollars and a microwave."

"Yeah. Tell about it."

"All right. I'll tell it." She finished her beer, then started into it. "Well, I'm at the auction one Friday and a fella that likes to hang around and tell everybody that everything's junk comes up to me and says, 'I want to buy your mule.' And I say, 'Mister my mule isn't here, and besides, I don't know if I want to get rid of it.' "

She was good about looking at everyone while she told it. And she had John Frederick from the word mule. He straightened up a little.

"But I hated that animal," she said. "So this man says, 'You don't ever work him. It's wasteful. I'll give you fifty dollars for him.' And I say 'a hundred dollars,' just for fun. And he gets real serious and says, 'I got to think about it.' Then he comes back a few minutes later holding a microwave and offers it and fifty dollars. So I accept and he pays me in ones."

Gid said, "Go on."

"So the next morning this fella pulls up with his trailer and goes out in the field. He lets the walk down and my mule goes in like it had been waiting for the man to come. And I can't believe it because that mule had never let anyone get near it. So I figure that maybe these two are a match. Before he pulls out he says, 'Hey. This animal got a name?' And I tell him Rubbermaid. And he says, 'Why the hell for?' but I don't tell him.

"Well, that afternoon he shows up at the stand and gets right up by my face shouting, 'I ought to kill you for what you done. I ought to knock your G.D. head off and I have a mind to do it.' When I don't say nothing, he says, 'Your mule kicked me in my liver lights. In my liver lights,' and he pointed like this. Now I don't know what liver lights are so I ask him, and he yells, 'It's where it's poisonous to get hit. You can die.' After a while he calms down and I ask him what he means to do about it. And he says, 'I already done it. I walked up to him and shot him in the G.D. face.' "

"You mean he shot it in the face?" John Frederick said. He spread his hands on the table. It was like he had been hoofed. We let him think about it.

"It was a bad mule," JoBell said.

"He won't work like he's supposed to?"

"He never worked a day."

It seemd to satisfy him. He sat back a little and put a piece of bread in his mouth.

"I got one too," Gid said. "Did I ever tell you about the boy I knew called Sparky? Fool who liked to shock himself?"

"Tell it, but tell it fast," JoBell said. "I got to go up by Roanoke tonight."

"All right. You'll like this one. I met this boy one time in Phenix City. He was doing some work on a friend of mine's house. My friend never really needed work done. He would just call this boy over for fun and pay him to rake the leaves or tighten spigots. My friend's one I worked with at the bank. Wasn't really a friend, I guess. I actually never really liked him. He was always talking about how nice his boat was, and how he had it dry-docked in the winter. I actually bitch-slapped him one time when he said something about my wife. I told him he would…"

"Who's this story about?" she said.

"I'm getting to it. Pass me that jelly. So this friend, or this boy I knew, he would always happen to have some people over because this boy of his liked to shock himself and he'd let anyone watch. A black man with blue eyes. Eyes as blue as berries. Damnedest thing I ever saw. And everyone called him Old Sparky because he'd unscrew a lightbulb and lick his finger and juke it up in there and sparks would shoot and his arm would shake and he'd start whooping and laughing. He'd go, 'whoo, whoo, ha, ha, whoo,' and then he'd undo a socket and grab the copper and do it all over. I saw him do it. And one time—I wasn't there but they swear it's true—they got him drunk and he says, 'I got one you ain't seen yet.' So he takes them outside and pops the hood on his old Scout. The motor's running and he undoes his fly and he lays his…he lays…well, he puts his peter right on the bumper. Then he grabs the nuts on the battery with both hands and his peter starts shooting sparks right off the metal and he's hollering and whooping and laughing."

We all sat quiet. That was it. I heard the clock ticking on the wall.

John Frederick said, "I knowed him. He was my baby's baby brother. We neber could tell what got into him. But she say to me that he been doing that shocking since he went to an electric schoolhouse."

"Your wife's brother?" Gid said.

"She hab the same blue eyes."

"You see I weren't lying," Gid said.

"Who said you were lying?" JoBell said.

"Well y'all ain't saying nothing. Sitting there like it weren't true."

"I believe it's true," she said. "But I don't know what to make of it."

John Frederick said, "Mister liked doing it. He did it when no one was there to see."

"Did you just say that he's your brother-in-law?" Gid said.

"Yes sir. But I habn't seen him since 1977."

JoBell cleared the plates and put some jelly on the table for dessert. I spread it on some bread with butter and folded it. Then she asked me if I would like to work with her for a little while.

I said I would.

10.

I STARTED MAKING THE EARLY DRIVES WITH HER TO ATLANTA, SLEEPING
most of the way. There was a big market at the fairgrounds where
all the growers sold, and by the time we were loaded up, light would
be yawning. It was slower coming back—the truck groaned under
the load and she didn't aim to work it to death. The long-haul rigs
would blow by and our course would quiver in their tail drafts. And
the sun came from behind us, as if to put a hand on our back and
chide us onward.

The first few days she made a game of getting me to talk. Maybe
she'd ask me what I wanted for supper, and I'd say, oh, anything. And
so she'd ask me to tell the things I would never eat and why not, but
I'd just say I'd eat any of it with salt. Or she'd ask me where I would go
if I could go anywhere, and then she'd have to admit that it was a bad
question. She didn't want to go anywhere either. But after a few days I
quit making like I was asleep. And maybe I'd ask her a thing or two.

At the stand I'd help her unload and do some chores. And at
night we'd ride out to work on the chimneys. I'd be up on the scaf-
fold catching and stacking the bricks. She'd be down below tossing
them over her shoulder like salt. I had to concentrate hard at first,
but after a few nights my hands worked without me. I'd notice how
the sweat spread like wings on her T-shirt and I'd watch her neck
twitch. The bricks floated up to me like bubbles until a stack was

finished. Then she'd straighten up and climb the metal.

I never did much after the stacking was done. I would hang my legs off the edge and watch the moths floating above the work light. They were like embers, and I wondered what they did before there was electricity or fire. I wondered if they headed for the moon.

After a couple of hours I'd go to the truck and slice some radishes. She said they kept her eyes sharp, and she taught me to like them on bread with two sides of butter and some salt. I'd carry them up to her.

"You got a job back home?" she asked one night.

"No."

"You know what kind you'd like?"

"They all seem the same. I'd do any of them."

"Well someone should pay you to sit around. You don't say much, but you make good company. My brother looked like you. He weren't as tall but he looked the same. He went to Vietnam."

"I could be a librarian," I said. "I wouldn't need a stool to get to the top shelf."

"You like books?"

"I like to look at them."

She thought for a minute. Her sandwich was on her lap, her handprints on the bread.

"I would read if I had time," she said. "I've never had time to do it much. And I wouldn't know which one to start with. I think I'm too far behind to catch up."

"Maybe if you didn't work two jobs."

"I don't know."

"Why do it anyway? Why do you brick these chimneys?"

"I used to do stone," she said. "But I fell a few years back. I can't swing the hammer like I used to."

It wasn't the first time I had asked her why she went so hard. But she wouldn't answer me straight. She just palmed her trowel and scraped her cuticles back.

———

Some weeks went by like that. Back and forth to Atlanta. Up and down the chimneys. We didn't hear much about the thing Gid had done. The first week she had read me a clip from a newspaper. It was the sheriff saying that Gid had lived his whole life in a twenty mile radius, and that men like him could never flee for good. He said he was expecting us to come walking back any day now, homesick. Then we didn't hear any more about it. We rode and worked and a full day could go by without me remembering why I was with her in the first place.

One morning she asked if I had voted for the tax. We had just picked up some coffee at a truck stop, and there had been lines of people from the counter to the beer fridges in the back. They wore uniforms from some factory, and the skin below their eyes hung like paper sacks of spilt coffee. They held their money in their fists.

I told her I didn't have a voting card. And I said, "You were against it?"

"No," she said. "But don't tell Gid I went for it."

"He doesn't mind. But why were you at the rally where you met him?"

"I hadn't made up my mind yet. I was trying to hear both sides. And you're right, when I got there and met him, I knew that the tax didn't bother him. His was a traveling preacher act, but I liked him."

"Why'd you go for it?"

"Well," she said. "In a couple of miles we'll cross into Alabama. And you could close your eyes and know when because the road will start to jolting you. I came to it one morning, a morning like this one. I had seen all them people in the Lotto line, and I knew that the dollars they held would keep the Georgia highway paved. And I wasn't for that—all the working people's dollars paving the highway. But I knew a state needs to get money somewhere or it can't keep up. So I decided that at least the governor's plan was better than Georgia's."

She pointed out the sign: "Welcome to Alabama."

"You understand?" she said.

"I don't know."

"You saw those people buying the tickets?"

I nodded.

"Those people just worked all night on their feet. Probably breathing rubber or burning their wrists on the line. And every one of them knows that one more dollar is one more chance to never work again. Work's tough so they spend their pay on a few chances in hell that they'll be able to kick their feet up until it's time to die. So their kids won't have to stand shoulder to shoulder with their coworkers' kids, breathing metal. And the government likes to tell everyone that the system helps poor kids go to college for free. But them people aren't fooled by that. The kids aren't gonna go to school. Only kids with As and Bs go on Lotto money. And them back there, their kids aren't making As and Bs because they're work-ing jobs at night to help out their folks. But they buy the tickets for one chance in hell. And their kids will do the same. And all of those dollars will keep those roads black. When I thought about that, I decided that at least our governor wanted the working people to pay less and the rich to pay a bit more, and that was fair enough."

She hardly ever got worked up. She laughed at herself and hummed a little. The highway was rough. It sounded like we were creeping over a cattle guard.

"But I've been meaning to ask you," she said. "Did you ever want to go to college?"

"I never wanted to go to kindergarten. Did you?"

"I went to college until my momma got sick. I was at Auburn for seven weeks."

"What'd you learn about?"

"I learned that most of the teachers were hiding out from something. I'd go to them if I didn't understand something, and they'd tell me everything about themselves and never answer my questions. I've always had that problem—people want to tell me every bad thing they've ever done. That's probably why I like you. You don't tell me nothing."

"There's nothing to tell. I've never done nothing."

"No one else has ever done nothing either," she said. "But they still tell you all of it."

11.

WE HEADED TO THE HOUSE ONE DAY WITH A SUMMER SAUSAGE AS BIG AS my thigh. A man had given it to us at the market in Atlanta, and all morning I'd been looking forward to watching Gid saw into the thing, to hearing him hum while he did it.

John Frederick was rocking on the porch when we pulled up. His clothes were hanging wet on the rail and he wore a towel. His beard had gotten thick. It was high on his cheeks and low on his neck and mostly white. I patted his shoulders, rolled and wound there like a sleeping mat on top of a backpack.

"Ebery cloud has blowed off," he said. "Yeah."

We looked up.

"Ain't that true?" he said. "That's right. And you know what else? My turnips are ready at the church. They hollering for me."

"Do you want me to take you back?" JoBell asked. "We can see you home."

"Nooo. I neber hab a home," he said. "But did you know that I draw a bath this morning. Yes sir. And I sat down in it and washed my pants and my shirt like they were my legs and my arms."

I sat in a rocker and looked at the light showing through the old man's clothes. JoBell went inside, then came out and knelt beside him.

"Mr. White," she said. "Did you see where Gid went?"

He nodded and rocked and kneaded his hands. She asked him again. He tried to talk again about his turnips, and it was a minute before we got him to tell us that Gid had woken up and drank a lot of beer. That he said he was going to walk up to Tennessee and buy some cigarettes. That he had gone out in the field and walked south towards the woods.

I handed JoBell the meat, hopped the fence and jogged across the meadow. I went along the tree line away from the highway. The next fence was at the top of a rise. I stood up on it and looked out. Far across the field, in the next corner, the cows were bunched up. I found Gid among them. His back was on the fence and he was making a speech.

"Mine is a thankless life," he was saying. "But let me say that if it weren't for me you'd be sold downriver so your man could pay more taxes. Your tongues, your hides, every part of you. And I'll only say it this once, bitches. But remember, who's the bull among you?"

Then he took on a kinder tone.

"I am not all that I say. I am not unlike you. Not for long, I mean. They're gonna lock me up too. I'll know how you feel then, beautiful ladies. You are all beautiful and your children will call you beloved. They won't be like all of mine. Everyone forgetting every nice thing I've ever done for them."

The cows nudged in.

I went around them and started to climb the fence. He saw me then.

"Junior. I've been waiting for you. Get these things away."

His overalls were caught on the wire. I took my time letting him loose.

"Where you going?" I asked.

"Just getting some air," he said. "I felt cooped up and needed to take a walk."

I fiddled with his overalls. "Where are you walking to?"

"Do I look like I'm walking anywhere? Concentrate, and don't rip them."

I had to hold him up on the walk back. He was apologizing every few steps. But he asked me to understand him too. He said it wasn't right that we should be living on the goodness of a woman— it was against the order of things—and so he had gotten drunk that morning just to blur the sight of his manhood abandoning him. I thought of leaving him in that field, saying things like that. I'd seen him eat from a woman's hand for too long. The thing that bothered him was that he didn't mind doing it, that this order of things he believed in had skipped him altogether.

I put him in the shower when we got back. We found the cans buried at the bottom of the trash. There wasn't any left in the fridge. JoBell said it would stay that way.

That night we sat on the porch and listened to the rain on the metal roof. Nobody was saying much. JoBell went inside and came back with a guitar. She tuned it and went to chording the strings and humming. And now and then the wind would catch some rain and mist us.

12.

GID GOT A LITTLE BETTER AND I WENT BACK TO MY ROUTINE. I'D SIT outside the stand and nod at the customers. When no one was around she would be in the doorway with her arms and legs crossed. The cars would pass and the nuts would drop and it was fine if we didn't speak for a long time. Then some out-of-towner would show up and want to know if pesticides had been used on the produce. And we'd laugh after the person had driven off without buying anything.

Or maybe, after some hours of nothing, she'd catch me looking after the girls who rode by in their boyfriends' trucks. The girls wore baseball caps and their hair blew around and they'd ash their cigarettes in the wind.

"I know that girl," she'd say. "She's no good."

"I give everyone a chance. I'm fair about it," I'd say. "And you shouldn't be so fast to tell all these men no."

She had a handful after her.

"Oh yeah," one guy said after a half an hour of wandering around. "I brought you these rattles from a diamondback. Just thought you'd like to see them. There's nine rattles there. The fella was four feet head to toe. Well, actually it was a female. Go ahead, take them. Them are for you. I got so many I don't have room for them no more. Just an old rattlesnake rattle, ain't nothing special about it. But I thought you'd like to see."

There were also a widower minister and a Little League ump. But I had an idea why she stuck to herself. One morning in Atlanta she had gone to see about some pecans when one of the growers started talking to me.

"Do you know whose sweater you're wearing?" he said. I shook no. "That's Dwight Esckridge's sweater. He gave it to her one morning in August when it went down to forty-two. We all saw him do it. Did you know him?"

"No sir."

"He grew oranges down near Muncy. Not too many trees but he knew how to get the most of them. Your friend always bought from him and he'd sneak an orange blossom in the grill of her truck sometimes. We all saw him do it and it made her crazy.

"Well it was foggier than hell one morning and Dwight never shows up. And he'd been here every morning since most of us were born. Older guy who could make anybody laugh without being too dirty and could sing every Elvis song—and some of them in French. When he doesn't show by six, Aunt Jo gets in her truck and heads out with her tailgate down. And it's still early. Some was still showing up. But she knew he'd be on time or something would be wrong. So she drives down 71 'cause this boy wouldn't take a freeway and she knows it. And she gets all the way to Tillman before she sees the wrecker hauling his truck off. You can believe that."

I told him I did.

"Ever wonder why she don't buy oranges?"

I had never thought about it.

———

On Friday afternoon two buses would go by. One with the football players, the other with the cheerleaders. JoBell used to go to the games but she didn't like the way they played anymore. There was too much passing for her.

"We's a country high school and we're trying to fun'n'gun," she said. "And what are you grinning at? You like those cheerleaders?"

"I like them all right."

She was in the doorway.

"I know two who might be good enough for you," she said. "I've been thinking about it."

We were eye to eye when I was sitting down.

"They're twin sisters. But they're only in the ninth grade. You'll need to wait on them."

"Do they ever come by?"

"Not much. I know them from church. I know their momma too. I don't think high school will spoil them."

"Church?"

"I go sometimes," she said. "Did you go?"

"No."

"You never went with Mr. White?"

"No. And he goes to black church."

"That doesn't matter."

"He never asked me to come."

"He probably thought you went to a different one. Anyway, I don't go much anymore. I don't think I've gone all year."

I nodded.

"It wouldn't be a bad idea for Gid to go once in a while," she said. "It can be helpful."

"I think it would mess him up."

"Why?"

"I think he'd start feeling bad about the thing he did and then he'd turn himself in."

"That's what he should do," she said.

"I don't know."

"No one can blame him for what he did. The court could blame him, but no one person. Of course he's blaming himself. He's roughing himself up so no one else can. That's why he should go to church. To feel clean."

"It's not the thing he did that's making him crazy," I said.

"How do you mean?"

"I don't know. But I think he's doing the same thing he's always done. He's trying to figure out why it went bad with her. He believes he messed up somewhere. That's why he roughs himself up. He's actually a little bit proud of the thing he did that night. I can tell when he's thinking about it. But it's all the stuff before that's getting him, just like it always has."

"You know better than me," she said.

"He hasn't been any different than he was before. Not any worse."

"Well it might be better he don't go then. It's hard to feel better when you don't know what you did wrong."

"Why did you quit going?"

She sat down beside me. The dog came to her but she sent him away.

"Why did I stop?" she said. "I guess I should tell you why I went. I went because I wanted to tell God that I wasn't upset with him anymore. But I couldn't do it."

13.

I TAKE MY TIME GETTING USED TO A GOOD THING, BUT I DO IT. SOME people might sabotage their own existence, might booby-trap their own homes, because they need a fight to feel alive. Well I ain't ever felt too alive, too high, or even that much at home. So I take any improvement that comes my way, and I don't ask for more. I keep it all in the middle. Now I was getting used to JoBell Bunting, used to the highway, used to the work. And it would have been fine if I kept on like that for a long time. If I never went to Birmingham or anywhere else. I had come far enough.

But then I was dozing at the stand one afternoon when a man pulled up in a truck and took a while getting out. He stopped before he went in and looked at me.

"You Tucker Phillips's boy?"

I said no. And he kept looking me. JoBell came to the doorway.

"Some fine produce, Miss Jo. Almost too good to be true. This late in the season. You have this stuff painted to look this bright. Ha."

She went inside and stood behind the counter. He followed her in and started telling her how well she ran her shop. But her prices were high, more power to her, so he got his vegetables from a little old man who liked to barter. She didn't say nothing. Then I only heard his boots on the floor. I heard him go over by the jellies, and back to the peaches, and up to the doorway. I saw him in the corner of my eye, through my hair. The dog looked up at him, and the man walked back inside.

"That man who came around with the clay governor before the referendum. You remember him, don't you?"

"Yeah. I remember him," she said.

"That's right. I saw you there talking to him. Second Sunday in August, if I remember. Well that boy came walking up to the station about a month ago. I thought he was suspicious, and familiar, to tell the truth, but I hadn't seen the story yet. Did you hear about him?"

"I heard."

"Shot a man who was in the backseat of his wife's car. He didn't die; the bullet went off his skull and into the seat, but that doesn't matter. And I've had a feeling that he ain't gone too far. I just got a feeling about it."

He stood in the doorway again. I looked down the road.

"We don't need any more criminals in this county. We got enough problem with the immigrants for our own people to be acting out too."

"You're not working today?" she asked.

"In a little bit." He walked around for a minute. "You gonna go down to the syrup sop next weekend?"

"I might go," she said.

"A lot more people go now but it's still the real thing. Those Loachapoka pickers been picking since I was a boy and I ain't too young. The boy with the banjo, the one who can play the wood saw, he gotta be near eighty. They sound good every year. I like the lady that grills the sweet corn and dips it right in the bucket of the darkest stuff she got."

"Aunt Sandy."

"Yeah. Fat Sandy. And there's always girls down there all sweet and hungry. I pray it's warm so they come out in shorts. But there again if it's crisp they need someone to keep 'em warm. Either way, they're better than the girls down in Dothan. It's not even worth the price of gas to go down there anymore. Most stuck-up girls in the world. Won't even let a guy talk to 'em. Peanut Festival's not at all what it used to be. I doubt if I'll ever go to Dothan again."

"I don't know about it," she said.

He stood above me for a minute before he left.

"Hey," he said.

I didn't look up.

When he had driven off, I started walking back. JoBell pulled up a minute later and waited for me to get in. I took a seat and didn't bother with the window. I watched the dust in the mirror.

Back home Gid and John Frederick were out on the porch. John Frederick was singing:

Don't let him catch you like he done before,
Skipping and dancing on the barroom floor,
Raising up trouble everywhere you go,
He's coming again so soon.
Be ready when he comes.

"He's been singing that for an hour," Gid said. "I'm starting to like it."

I went inside.

"Junior?" Gid called after me.

I rolled up the old man's blanket and came back out.

"We got to go," I said.

John Frederick stood up. Gid just looked at us.

"Fella that works down the road at the station came by and said he heard about you. He recognized Merit," JoBell said.

Gid went inside and came out holding his shoes.

"I knew it weren't good for you to be down there all the time," he said.

John Frederick got in the front seat and we climbed in the bed. I watched her house as we bumped down the drive. Gid lay his head down on the spare tire.

"Go ahead and lay down," he said.

We headed west. Gid had told her to drive us to Lake Martin and let us out by the fishing camps. We crossed the counties and I pulled my arms inside my shirt to keep warm. We came to a market that sold live bait. She stopped by the payphone and cut the motor.

14.

WE HAD GOTTEN FAR AWAY AND NOW IT WAS AFTERNOON IN A STRANGE place. The rush was gone out of us. I squatted on my haunches and set the blanket on the pavement. I kept going back to her stand and her truck and our dirty fingerprints on the sandwich bread, thinking, we should have never met that woman. And she had driven off so easy. Before I knew her, I had things buried away. Things I had buried and forgotten about. You can do that, same as you can bury a lunch box of Indian money when you're a kid and not ever find it again. But now I had those things back. And I'm too old to bury things anymore.

The pay phone rang. John Frederick went right for it, and put his hand on his other ear.

"It's a woman," I said. "Look. He took his hat off."

Gid shrugged and went for the store. The old man listened for a long time.

"Oh. Oh, I see. Well yes. That is bad. Yes ma'am."

Gid came back and let him know we were leaving.

"That's mighty nice of you to say so," John Frederick was saying. "That's right. We should get together and go for a ride. But my car's blowed up and my driber's license been dead for a long time. You in North Carolina?"

We followed Gid up the road. It was an old gray road without lines. We were shaded by old pines, and through the trees, down the hill, there was the lake. When the breeze came sighing through the needles, it sounded like a car coming, and Gid kept looking over his shoulder.

"You got any ideas, Junior? Old man? What do you think?"

"These are fishing camps?" I said.

"They used to be," Gid said. "Ten years ago they were. But they've knocked them down so all these rich people can build these secondary homes. And ain't nobody in them this time of year. What do you think it would hurt to go in one and stay a while?"

"I don't worry about where I'll sleep, or what I'll eat or wear. I think about the birds flying," John Frederick said.

"The hell does that mean?"

"I'b gone to sleep ebery day of my life and woke the next day safe and sound. That's true. Yeah. It is."

"Glad to hear it," Gid said. "And I'm not worried either. But I don't think God would want a house sitting empty while good people don't have a place to lay down. You agree, Junior?"

I did.

The road ended soon. There were a few houses by the water with paved driveways and brick mailboxes. Gid said that we should try for the last one, so we went in the woods and along the foot of a hill towards the water.

"There's a car home," Gid said when we were even with it. "But I know this kind. They'll leave a vehicle just to pull their boat when the weather's warm. There's nobody there."

I wasn't sure, so we sat down and watched. The gusts from the lake took the leaves off the ground, swarmed them across the hillside, and sprayed them against the trunks, and the noise was loud and constant, like bacon grease in a hot pan. I could hardly hear John Frederick sing. Maybe an hour went by.

"All right," Gid said. We brushed our pants off. "There's nobody there. Me and the old man will stay back. Junior, you go to that side door and break one of the panes. We'll come when you get in."

I looked at him.

"Okay, then. Maybe I'll do it," he said. "I'll do every damn thing."

He ducked through the yard and along the wall to where the truck was parked under the porch. Then he disappeared for a second and came back with a canoe paddle.

"He's gonna do it. Hey. Yes sir. Found him a weapon," John Frederick said.

Gid spread his legs in front of the door and raised the paddle. He pulled it back several times, like a pool cue. The glass broke easily enough and he turned towards us to wave. Then an alarm rang out. Gid ran across the yard and stomped into the woods. I reached down for John Frederick. He had taken a seat and he was saying something very fast. I helped him up.

We went marching through the forest with Gid a ways ahead. The old man breathed ugly. He stared up through the trees and didn't watch where he was stepping. Gid kept telling us to come faster. I pulled the old man along. Foam thickened at the corners of his mouth. We went across a hill and down the other side. We were getting further and further from the water. The alarm still sounded, but we were far enough away to hear our footsteps. Gid slowed down. We leaned against a big tree. John Frederick's eyes were foggy. His nose ran over his mustache.

"You think we've gone far enough?" Gid asked.

"Yeah," I said.

"Rich people."

"Yeah."

I sat beside the old man and closed my eyes. A breeze came steady up the hillside. It cooled me through. When I opened my eyes I saw that night was coming early.

"You got any ideas?" Gid asked me.

"Not any good ones."

"Did she give you any money?"

"Yeah. But I left it at the house."

"I think I stepped on a thorn. But I don't want to look."

"Sit down then," I said.

But he kept walking around. He went tree to tree, leaning on one for a second, then on another, like pressure on the right spot might open up a door in the wood, and he could walk deep inside the hill to a motel bedroom with a cable TV and a Bible with his name on it.

"We probably didn't even need to hurry," he said. He sat beside me. "Police will just think it was some kids."

"It was a nice stroke."

"What?"

"Breaking that window."

"Did I ever tell you about that woman who threw her boots through my daddy's window?"

"Yeah."

"I need a cigarette or something. I'm all jumpy." He cupped his hands and breathed into them. "Old man I apologize for making you hurry like that. Next place we come to we'll get you hitched on a ride home."

I scooted away from the tree and lay down. The birds and squirrels made a lot of noise getting ready for night. I watched a yellow leaf fall. It blew around and landed on the old man's hat. He was sleeping.

Gid saw it too. He said, "Old man, you're a good person. If you know secrets for being the way you are, I'd like to hear."

When night came, we lay against each other and pulled the blanket over our heads. That way our breath could keep our faces warm. Gid said that we were like enchiladas under there. Then it was hard to think about anything but food.

15.

IN THE MORNING THERE WAS THE COLD SMELL OF BURNING WOOD, THE way smoke can only smell in fall. A mourning dove called. Gid rolled out from the blanket. He went to a tree and steam rose from his stream. He shivered once, buttoned himself up, and put his hands in his pockets. John Frederick coughed hard a few times and rolled onto his side.

The leaves were frosty. They chirped under our feet as we walked. The smoke got harsher. We rounded the crown of a hill and found a guy sitting in a lawn chair by a small fire. Now it is never a casual thing to find another man in the forest. Under the trees is a kingdom of animals, which is to say, a kingdom where killing is lawful, and a man understands this when, through the trees, he sees a stranger. It is not unlike the presence of a copperhead curled on your path. You think about the end. So it wasn't right that this guy laughed when he saw the three of us. It wasn't right that he took a long drink of beer as if to allow us the time to consider him. Him, with red, ropy forearms and a jaw like a Mustang fender. We stopped and looked at each other. The man got up. Gid started my way, and at the same time, I started his. The man swayed.

"Three of us is lost," he said. "Some but not all. You can call me Rodney Jones."

He found his balance and walked behind one of a few tarps

strung tight in the trees.

"Let's go," Gid whispered. But the guy was already back.

"Here," he said. "A chair for the tired travelers. Travelers."

He unfolded some lawn chairs. Then he kicked opened an old suitcase and took out a couple cans. He gave one to me and one to Gid. John Frederick said no. I took a seat beside the old man. But Gid just stood there.

"Sit on down," the man said. "Your legs are twitching. Like you're tired. I heard y'all coming for a half an hour. It was so slow I knew you wouldn't be the law. You're lost pretty good."

"We're not lost," Gid said. "We're just doing some hiking."

The man snorted. I opened my beer and took a nice swallow. And the guy kept smiling, looking at Gid, then looking at me.

"I went hiking last night," he said finally. "I took some cans and threw them at a truck and they didn't even stop. No one wants to fight anymore or have any regular fun. I got up on the road with a willow branch but not one vehicle came for an hour. It weren't even that late but no one stays out anymore."

"That's right," Gid said, and he stole a glance my way. "People are scared."

"Everybody is. They all think I'm gonna take their money or their wife or their vehicle. Rich people spy me with a handful of water snakes and they think I worship the devil. No one has any fun anymore because they're nervous for the things they have that might get away. Even the one's who got nothing are scared now. It used to be the simple people could laugh easy and party the best. But not now. And most of the girls won't either. They're worried they'll get poisoned."

I couldn't tell if he was drunk or if drinking for a long time had made him that way.

"How far are we to town?" Gid said.

"You're lost pretty good."

"Not lost. Just gonna hike until we come out the other end."

"Fifteen miles to town. Or three if you know the way."

"We know that way. Is this a hunting camp you got?"

"I've been in this spot since summer. It's almost time to move."

Then it looked like he would laugh again.

"Y'all's running away, aren't ya?" he said.

I wanted to get away from the guy. Every minute that passed seemed like another day since we had been at JoBell's. It had been a fine routine, and I got to remembering the man who had run us off. Connie Bivens. And I thought it would be good to go back to his gas station with a pack of matches. Before he came around I could pluck an apple off the table anytime I was hungry. I'd cut a green one up and dip it in the peanut butter she kept under the counter. Then I had showed up and he had to be cute about it. He had circled me like some pink, feather-plucked bird.

Then I remembered another thing. Something he had said after I stopped listening. "He didn't die; the bullet went off his skull and into the seat, but that doesn't matter. He's still a criminal."

I heard it again and again. And I told myself I was making it up. But his words were like a brush with poison ivy. A day later it shows and spreads and you cannot say it didn't happen. His words crawled all over me.

"No sir," Gid said. "We're just enjoying the weather. Hiking."

"Big reward?"

"Mister," Gid said. "We ain't done nothing."

"One of you has."

"Listen. We're upstanding. And we're proud of that. Thanks for letting us sit and rest. Come, Junior." He acted like he would get up, and he took another drink.

"I wouldn't turn the law on to nobody," Rodney Jones said. "The way they've chased me through these woods, shooting after me like I was game, and all I ever done never amounted to a killing. I wouldn't do it for all the girls in Cuba."

"You know about Cuban girls?" Gid said.

Rodney Jones crushed his can in his fist and took another. "Sit for a minute. I never get to say the things I got to say."

I kept at my beer. It was working fast down my neck and across the top of my wrists. It was getting Gid too. Soon he let a laugh slip out before he could get his hand up.

Then he asked, "You do all right with girls up here?"

Rodney Jones just grinned.

"Because I used to do all right myself," Gid said. "Running around. It wasn't many said no."

"I don't even ask. They come at me. They want to tame what's wild."

"That's true. But don't let them do it. They get you in this cage and they only let you out when they need you. And they pick at your brain for fun."

"Who can tame me?"

"Well," Gid said. "You might be safe up here. But I used to say the same thing. Then I let one inside my brain and she picked at it till I felt crazy. I was crazy too. She tamed me over time, a little bit here, a little more there, and I didn't know until she had me all chained and twisted up. You know how you fake a dog by acting like you're throwing a ball? That's how they do it."

Our host tossed us some beer. "You running from her grip?" he said.

"I'm not running," Gid said. "That was a long time back. I got a good one now."

"Maybe you cut her," he said and made his finger like a knife and drew a smile across his neck.

I figured they wouldn't lock Gid up forever. Maybe a few years, then parole. I could get up in court and say that she had ruined him on purpose. They would be divorced, and when he got out, it could be just like it should be: me and Gid and John Frederick, and no more of this wandering. I wanted to get away and tell him, but we weren't in any shape to leave.

Gid was spinning his beer in his hands, studying it like a piece of pottery. He opened it and drank it down straight.

"I'm not running," he said again.

Rodney Jones tossed him another and continued what would be an entire day of women talk: boasting, lament, relationship theory, biology.

"When I was in the Army, they put me in South Korea," he said. "And those little girls loved American soldiers. They'd talk at me all soft and high and I'd take them off to do it. And they loved it more than I did. And there was one named Cindy that I asked to come home when I got out. I was ready to work for my daddy and look after her. But when I asked her, down there on my tore-up knee, she just laughed. So I shook her by the throat until she was blue almost. And when I let her go, she got her breath and laughed some more. And I left her in her shitty little concrete apartment house, and when I got in the street, I heard her laughing through the window."

Then he pulled his pant leg up and showed us a scar. He said he meant to play linebacker for Troy State, but his high school girl was driving the ski boat and she pulled him into a stump and his knee went the wrong way.

"We'll stay for a beer or two," Gid said. "But we got to be back for supper tonight. My lady's making us an Italian feast. She's Italian."

"I'm done with foreign girls. They always have to take charge. They want to tell you how to do everything."

"Not my lady," Gid said. "She likes to please me every way she can. Italian women are different because they're brought up different. They're part Catholic, the good part. My lady likes to watch me eat. She kisses me when my mouth's full and she calls me Popi."

———

When night came so did the rain. The four of us sat under the bedroom tarp. I had sobered up, and I sat beside John Frederick thinking about food. The old man had his hands folded on his lap and his feet crossed. He smiled at the darkness. The rain had been getting through in places. It kept hitting my leg, and when the old man noticed, he set his hat there to catch it.

The other two were telling stories whose endings were mixed up or forgotten. The one about the gal with hair down to her butt. The lie about the willing sisters. I had stopped listening before it got dark.

"I'm gonna go rambling," Rodney Jones said suddenly. "You coming with me? Catch some bad girls."

"Where you find them?" Gid said.

"Anywhere."

"Better stay back tonight. I don't need any more trouble than I got."

"You come with me, young fellow?"

I told him I had blisters. Rodney Jones stood up, took a step forward, rocked back, then walked a few steps out in the rain. He turned around and I could see the white of his smile.

"Would it be okay if we stayed here tonight?" Gid said.

"If you don't rat me, I won't rat you."

He was gone then, and we could hear him whooping down the hill.

There were several blankets lying around. We didn't need to lie as close as the night before. Gid was snoring right off. I tried shutting my eyes but my stomach was torqued. I thought about a scoop of macaroni and cheese on top of a slab of country ham. I thought of raw macaroni, and I pretended I was crunching it in my mouth. I rubbed my teeth together. Then I licked at my thumbnail. It was salty underneath. I did it to all of my fingers. I was thinking of rummaging through the other tarps for something to eat when John Frederick held his finger up.

"I only hab one woman in my life," he said. "I found her in a bean patch and we got married the next day. She gib me her hand

and I take it and I hold on because she was something wild. But you know she always come to church. She always say her prayers even if she drunk. I knowed she was good when I find her because her eyes lined up. That's true. We got married at the church. But when she not come home, Mr. Police tell me I neber was her husband and she neber was my wife because we neber got official at the courthouse. And I said that we were married before God and he was the judge. Then, when they put in the paper that she was lost, they wrote her down as Lorna Doone Nail instead of Lorna Doone White."

A raindrop hit him in the eye. I put his hat on his face. He pulled it away and said, "Listen to that water hitting that sheet. When it does like that you can believe that somebody's leabing home foreber. A soft rain will let you know."

Those were the only words he had said all day. The rain tapered off then. Not a lot of drops fell through.

16.

GID WOKE UP NEAR SOBER AND HAD COFFEE BY THE FIRE. HE DRANK IT
fast and poured some more.

"Where is he?" he said, wiping some from his chin.

"He said he was going to see his daddy," I said. "Tell him he loves
him."

"Well, we better walk on. That guy isn't right."

"Eat some of these potatoes," I said. "He made them for us."

"I'm not saying he's evil. But he's not right either," Gid said.

"Well c'mon."

He slung his coffee on the fire, and we left. But as we were going
down the hill, I remembered the blanket. I ran back for it and took
another one too. Gid led the way. He was always looking around,
jerky, like he thought that man was gonna be standing on the other
side of some tree.

We found an old wire fencerow soon enough and decided we
could follow it to civilization. As we went along I prepared to tell
Gid that he hadn't killed that boy like he thought.

Gid, I thought, *that man that was doing it to Robyn, he's still
alive. You missed him somehow. You took off part of his ear, maybe.*

But I didn't say it. I figured I'd wait and see where we ended up.

"How's your head?" I asked.

"It don't feel bad but it's early still. My shoes are coming apart though. The damn heel is about to start flapping."

"Not mine," John Frederick said. "I'b been wearing these for years and years. When Moses and the peoples walked in the desert their shoes neber wear out. And the childrens' shoes grew with their feet. And for forty years their shoes stay together. There weren't no shoemakers in the desert. So God kept their feet shod himself."

"Yeah," Gid said. "Well what about the babies that were born? Did they come out wearing sandals?"

"They may hab. Yeah. I neber thought about it."

We came out on a road and followed it downhill. The blacktop was new and the stray paint looked like pollen beside the fresh yellow lines. It was good to put my feet on something sure. I walked out in the middle, feeling strangely high.

But we rounded a curve and saw the lake. And there were more big houses, bigger than the one we had tried to camp in. I knew that they were empty, with covers on their pool tables and Jacuzzis. It ruined the walking for me, and I thought it would be nice to burn the whole street.

But first I thought I'd like to go to a party on a lawn, like the ones in the catalogs, just to see what they're like. There'd be floral seat cushions and cut flowers and glass pitchers of real lemonade. And skewers of chicken and grilled corn and every girl with a white dress and a college diploma.

"Watch you don't get barbecue sauce on your dress, Sarah," some woman would call from the deck.

"Mom, go back inside with your friends."

There'd be shrimp with cocktail sauce and a crystal dish for the tails. The girls wouldn't smoke but the boys would. And they'd hold their beers in insulated cushions.

"You know what I call these things, Brett?" one would say. "I call 'em titties."

"What the hell for?"

" 'Cause they're soft and you hold them."

"Good one, Cheever. That's good. I like that one."

I'd wear a khaki suit and my Velcro shoes, and drink a mint julep from a silver cup. Then I'd have another and walk with a girl to the dock to lay down and stop the spinning. Just lay on the splinter deck in my new suit because I'll get a new one next summer. And there was too much bourbon in that drink but who cares, because tomorrow's Sunday.

"You gonna work for your daddy's firm, Merit?" she'd say.

"I don't know. Probably not for a while. I might go out to Colorado, hang out for a while. Work in a ski shop in Vail. I'm not in any hurry to have a real job. But yeah. I'll probably go to law school."

"Will you stay in Birmingham?"

"I don't know. I might go to Atlanta. There's more going on there."

"Atlanta? I like shopping there. But I could never leave Birmingham."

"You know if I had a reason to stay in Birmingham, I would."

It would be nice to do all that for a weekend. Leave my shoes and dishes around for someone to pick up. Go skiing on the lake with a bunch of beer. Then, when everyone went back to Birmingham, I'd walk down the street with a can of kerosene and a box of matches. I'd paddle out in an inner tube and watch them glow. The trees would catch fire too.

We walked past fifty houses. Most of them had gates.

"Mansions," John Frederick said.

No cars passed us. No dogs barked. Nobody was around. I kicked a crumb of asphalt for a while. Then a squawking broke.

"Geeses," John Frederick said. He was pointing. "Look how they do. They make a B with their king at the front."

"C'mon," Gid said.

We turned away from the lake and went down a county road. Then the pavement was gray, and there were trailer places near the road with fat women on the porches. And there'd be babies and dogs around and a lot of stuff crammed under the porch. John Frederick took his hat off every time he saw one. He'd stop and wave and Gid would tell him to hurry the hell up.

The smaller the roads we walked, the more we saw signs protesting the governor's tax plan. It had been almost two months since the vote and the papers had said that another attempt at a tax hike would wait ten years or more. It would be that long before some politician forgot that minds can't be changed. But the signs stayed up like trophies.

Gid stopped at one. He kicked at the stakes for a minute, then pulled the thing free, and threw it in the weeds. We kept on.

A while later he said, "There was that Auburn man who came to Loachapoka to humble me. Brought all his students with him. Skinny little bastard with a caved-in chest. I told you about him? Well, I was gonna kick him around. But I got this feeling he was right about how the tax would end up helping the poor folks. I hadn't given any thought to it. But the next day I felt like maybe I was getting everyone riled up against something that was maybe gonna help them out."

He pulled a weed, tasted the end, and threw it back down.

"Like we were all a bunch of wounded dogs trying to bite our owner," he said. "Anyway. When it came to it, I forgot to vote."

"I gib to the man whateber he tells me to gib," John Frederick said. "If a coin got Abraham Lincoln's head on it, then I let Abraham Lincoln hab it."

"Yeah, old man? That's considerate." Gid said. "Junior, I forgot to tell you. The Braves got swept by the Cubs in the first round. I saw the paper at a quickie mart. Lost three straight and only one was close. An artichoke's got more heart than the Atlanta Braves. The paper said they were laughing in the dugout in game three. They don't give a damn. They're just happy to go back to Florida and play golf for a few months. Won the pennant for twelve years and they only got one ring. Andruw missed batting practice because he was playing a video game and eating wings. And Chipper hasn't been good since he knocked up that Hooters waitress. I think she gave him AIDS. He looks so pale."

"They should put him back at third."

"Auburn's been winning though. Beating up on Vandy and a bunch of nobodies. We're 5-2 and the paper said Cadillac's been player of the week for about a month. We'd be 2-5 without that boy and you know he'll just go turn pro at the end of the year. Poor kids always leave early."

Then he started into a bit about Robyn. He did it for the same reason, saying how wrong it was that he should be stuck with a heartless wife and a couple of gutless teams.

I wondered what Robyn was doing. If the grass was high in the yard or if she had gone out and cut it herself. The choke was broken. She couldn't have figured it out. I pictured her happy with the attention she was getting. Making herself out to be a victim of another loveless marriage. Saying she was only sleeping with that councilman because he understood her and it was awful, Honey, living with a man with no ambition. Then I saw her sitting in her car replaying the thing Gid did. I wondered if she could still hear the gunshot. She was probably having bad dreams. She was probably standing in front of the mirror a lot, spraying perfume and considering the droop of her chest.

17.

CARS WOULD COME SLOW PASSING SOMETIMES, BUT IT WASN'T MANY
that offered a ride. We'd nap in ditch weeds, bed by the fence lines,
and hope against rain. It wasn't much to take food from a grocery.
I'd buy one thing and leave with five. And we'd go back to walking,
which is a fine thing to do if you got nowhere to be.

During the long silences I would think of Florida. I'd seen ads
for work on the oil rigs. I could work half the month and make
more than a banker. And we could have a backyard where the old
man could plant and water. Florida, I decided. Grapefruit. And we
kept north.

One afternoon a deputy stopped to see if we were okay. Gid
told him we were doing great. The guy said to enjoy the weather,
and as he started driving off, I thought, *ain't nobody really looking
for us.* We were a lot of things, but I didn't think *wanted* was one.
And even if I was wrong, even if some guy in a cruiser four counties away had some memory of the thing Gid did, even remembered the governor statue and all that, we had a decoy in tow. I'd
been noticing that the plain sight of John Frederick was the main
curiosity anywhere we went. People would stare into his scaly eyes
or study his warped shape, even while they talked to us.

Still, I wouldn't have done what Gid did next. As the cruiser was
pulling away, he spied an Auburn bumper sticker and let out a "War

Eagle." The car stopped and the guy stuck his head out the window. "You're darn right. War Eagle," he said.

Gid walked up to his window and shook his hand. And after a minute I was in the back with John Frederick and Gid was riding shotgun. Officer Berry was talking all about himself. His uniform was new. He worked for a lady sheriff. He was in the National Guard and it looked like he could be sent to Iraq. He hoped so. His momma and daddy were retired from the postal service. Daddy delivered the mail on a horse at the beginning. And they were always wishing they could have people over for supper more. Would we like to come tonight?

"What's that?" Gid said. He hadn't heard a word.

"You three are welcome for supper."

"That's all right. That's all right," Gid said. He pushed his fists in the seat and sat up a little straighter. "I mean, that's friendly. But it's all right."

"Where you going anyway?"

"Well, I'll tell you. I got a cousin, a first cousin, who just moved up here. We're going to see him. Can you roll this window down for me?"

"You got it, friend. Where you coming from?"

"Lee County."

"On your feet?"

"No," he said, trying for a laugh. "Not on our feet. My wife was driving but we got in a little fight on the way. She pulled over and told us to get out."

"It was a bad fight?"

"Not too bad. But I thought we were closer to town."

"You look like you've been at it a while. Don't worry though. I'll take you to his house. What road's he on?"

"Just since this morning," Gid said, and he put his hand to his face, measuring his stubble. "He told us to call from town and he'd come get us."

"Well, it's a shame they haven't got us our cell phones yet," the deputy said. "We were supposed to have them by now but they ain't coming 'cause the tax didn't go through. I'm not saying I was for it, but it would have made our work easier. We'll let you use the phone at the station."

I imagined that when we got there some thin-lipped man would try to bully me into a confession. Maybe they'd separate us all and that would be the end of life with Gid for a while. I put my knees against the divider and sunk down in the thought. And it wasn't altogether bad. But I did have a few things I wanted to tell him, things I'd always figured I'd say one day. But if this was it, if I didn't get a chance? Well then maybe I'd find that councilman in Phenix City and finish the thing, as some sort of thanks.

We pulled into town. There was a big square with a lot of storefronts. They wore faded awnings like old visors, and their vacant windows gazed hollow across the square. The courthouse was in the middle. It was red and good-looking, strong. We parked and went in. There was a nice-looking receptionist in the sheriff's office chewing gum and twisting her hair around a pen. We followed the deputy to his office. He showed us the phone. Gid dialed a number and looked at me.

"Ain't nobody picking up," he said. He was sweating pretty good.

"Try it again," the deputy said.

Gid dialed again and waited. "He ain't there."

"You have the right number?"

"Yeah. I memorized it."

"I could look him up in the phone book and take you over there."

"No," Gid said. "He won't be in there. He just moved up a couple weeks ago. He drives a truck. Maybe they sent him on a long haul and he forgot to tell me."

The receptionist brought a file to the deputy. He thanked her and set it on his desk.

"Well, supper will be ready in twenty minutes," he said. "You can try and reach him from Momma and Daddy's."

Gid said that would be nice. He wanted out of there. Outside he told me to sit in front. He got in the back and cracked the window.

"What's she making tonight?" I asked.

"I don't know," the deputy said. "Are you hungry?"

"A little."

We went north for a few miles. The deputy unbuttoned his shirt collar and turned the radio on. He waved to everyone that passed. Then John Frederick leaned forward and stuck his hand in the front seat.

He said, "I got to say something I might hab neber said."

He held a driver's license with the plastic peeling back at the corners. He touched it to the deputy's shoulder. The deputy took it.

"Born in 1929," he said. "You want me to believe you're that old."

"Well, that is true," John Frederick said. "But it also says there that that license has been dead eleven years. And all that time I dribe with it in my pocket. And I know a crime is a crime eben if you don't know you're doing it. Just like a sin is a sin eben if you don't know it's a sin. And I feel bad about the crime I did eben though I didn't know it was one. And I'm ready to pay whateber price I got to pay. You a good man. And I won't eat at your table with a stain on my mind. I wouldn't lift my fork. No sir."

The deputy looked at me. Then in the rearview.

"Buddy," he said. "Just you sit back and take it easy. Your expired license don't concern me."

"Oh yeah? Why do you say it?"

"You're not driving this car, are you?"

"No sir. I'm riding it."

"That's right. So as long as I don't catch you driving, you're not in any trouble."

The deputy was smiling. He handed me the license. I put it in my pocket.

The Berry's driveway was a circle of dirt. We pulled around and two dogs ran alongside the deputy's door.

"Get back girls," he said. "Let me out."

We got out and the dogs sniffed John Frederick. He turned a circle. Berry pointed to a trailer next to the house. "That's where I stay," he said. "Never got too far from home, I guess." The woman came out the front door and waited for the dad to step over the doorsill. She was holding his hand.

The deputy went up the stairs, kissed his mother, and shook his dad's hand in big circles. They laughed, and I got the feeling they always did it that way.

"Come on up," the deputy told us. "I brought some friends for supper. This here's…"

"I'm Patty Berry. We're glad to have you." She stuck her hand out to Gid. He took it and said, "Ma'am, my name's Red. And I'm glad to be here."

"Red what?" her husband shouted.

"Red White," Gid said, and he couldn't keep from shaking his head.

"Merit White," I said, and shook their hands.

"And I'm Mr. John Frederick Templeton White, and I'm seventy-four years old and I plow them."

They held the storm door for us. Inside I smelt something roasting. The floors were almost black and the entry was dark. Samuel Berry stopped and opened a door. He turned the light on and handed me a bar of soap and a hand brush.

———

I ate for a long time that night. I mixed the chicken in my mashed potatoes, poured the gravy on top, and let it run over into the corn and beans. I kept smelling me, smelling Gid and John Frederick, and kept trying see if our hosts had caught it too. We needed a bath. That was plain. But they just carried on like we were family, maybe family you don't show off, but family still.

Mr. Berry was so loud and happy and frail.

"Sammy, I caught your ma in a crime today," he said.

"What'd she do this time?" the deputy said.

"Well, I woke up from my nap and I seen her with a glass of ice water headed for the back door."

"But Ma doesn't take ice in her water."

Patty Berry was blushing.

"That's right. She never has. So I asked her what she wanted with a glass of ice water and she said, 'Oh, nothing.' And I said, you better tell me or I'll go ahead and die and make you a widow. And do you know what she told me that ice water was for?"

"What?"

"For our rooster," he shouted.

"Well, he won't drink water anymore if it don't have ice," she said. She was embarrassed, and she dabbed her eyes with her napkin. "I gave it to him in August and he just got used to it."

I cleaned my second plate with a hot roll. I slouched in my chair and listened to the family telling stories. I wondered if they told the same ones every night. Or if they had certain stories for certain dishes. They never shut up.

I helped the deputy clear the plates. We stood by the sink, and after he had scrubbed one, I toweled it off. He thanked me after every one. John Frederick was in the middle of a long story that didn't make sense. Something about a tractor that caught fire in the rain when it wasn't even running. The story went on and on, and when he was finished, Mr. Berry was asleep in his chair.

"I'll fix you boys a place to sleep," the mother said. "We got plenty of room. Samuel's brothers built him this house when we got married. We put four rooms in it because we figured on having a mess of children. But only Sammy came."

"I should try my cousin again," Gid said. "We should stay with him."

The deputy showed him to the phone.

"He ain't picking up," Gid said.

"Well, you can try him in the morning, and if he's still not around, then maybe your lady will want you back. At least you have a lady. I can't find a good one around here."

I went with Mrs. Berry to help get the beds ready. But they were already made. All she did was turn the sheets down and fluff the pillows. She told me all about the Ashland Tigers and their game with Lineville on Friday. They always played at the end of every season and she had seen every game in her seventy-one years. Even the one in the rain when she was due to have Sammy. She knew that Ashland would win this year because they had a better defense. She said she liked the team because there wasn't a standout player like Lineville had. Just eleven boys who played hard. We went in the other room and two jerseys hung on the wall above the bed. One was cotton and the other was mesh. They were both number 67. "Samuel and Sammy both hiked the ball," she said. "There was no glory for them in the trenches but they sure liked it in there. Pushing and clawing all night."

Before she left, she asked me if I would come to the game. The way she asked, it was like she knew we'd be staying.

Gid took the big bed and me and the old man got the smaller ones in the other room. While I crawled in, he went to the window and sang.

Daddy in the henhouse, momma on the rail,
Looks like a rain but it's not gonna hail,
If I lose my money, let me lose. If I lose my money let me lose.
Lose your money, Baby, don't lose your mind.
Lose your money, don't you mess with mine.

I turned the lamp off, kicked the covers off my feet, and listened to him go.

18.

JOHN FREDERICK WAS AT THE TABLE WITH GRAVY ON HIS BEARD AND AN open Bible before him. He was working through it back to front, and reading the page numbers aloud. I took a seat and the mother gave me a plate.

"Your daddy's not feeling well," she said. "He's on the sofa with a big, thumping headache. Says it hurts to open his eyes up. He can't get a hold of his cousin and your momma won't pick up the phone either. But don't you worry. You just pretend you're at home."

I found Gid stirring on the couch. He was restless.

"I can't go to the game, Junior," he said real quiet.

"What?"

"I told her we might stay another night. Then she said we had to go to the game with them tonight. The tailgate and all."

"Too many faces?"

"That's right," he said. "The whole damn county will be there. I'd tell them we had to walk on but we'd freeze."

I didn't know if he was right. I thought that maybe people would recognize the clay governor sitting in the stands but not the man who made him. Gid didn't look any different from anybody else.

I sat in the kitchen and watched the lady work. She kept having me taste the stew to tell her if it had enough flavor. She pretended she was very worried about it. John Frederick sat there with the Bible. He had found the maps at the back.

"Are you a preacher, Mr. White?" she asked him.

"No ma'am. I plow fields back and forth. But I might be a preacher in heaben. You neber know what your job gonna be there."

"My daddy was a preacher."

"He was?"

"Yes. And so was my granddaddy. My brother was gonna be a preacher too but he died in Korea. I got four sisters and two of them are married to preachers. One's a Methodist and the other's a Pentecostal, but I don't know about all that."

She went to check on Gid.

"Not all preachers gonna go to heaben," John Frederick told me. "Just like not all murderers are gonna burn."

The mother came back.

"I believe he's a little worse," she said. "When the weather changes like this it can get you."

She washed her hands and dried them on her apron.

"Did you play football, Merit?"

"I homeschooled."

"Your momma taught you?"

"Yes ma'am."

"When Sammy played, those were the best years of my life. I was sadder than he was after his last game. They beat a Christian school for the state championship. They played it at the Iron Bowl on the fake grass. We beat them 26 to nothing and I cried for a week. Sammy got his championship ring sized to his pinky and gave it to me when it came. I'm gonna wear it tonight."

She turned around and stirred the pot.

"Where did you grow up, Mr. White?" she asked.

"Beside Stapleton," he said. "I went to the fifth grade and my teacher told me I would be a teacher too. But I started in the field beside my daddy when I was ten."

———

The deputy came home before dark. He woke his dad up from a nap and helped his mom pack the cooler. He put a letter jacket on and said he had gotten too fat. Then Mrs. Berry called the family in the hallway. They whispered. I went to check on Gid. He rolled his eyes.

Sammy came in first. His parents were holding hands behind him.

"Ma's gonna stay and take care of Red," he said. "She wants to watch and make sure he doesn't get worse.

Gid was on his feet. "No. I'm doing a little better. It's wearing off."

But he stood up too fast and kind of fell onto the couch. They didn't believe him.

"No," the old man said. "You're not well."

I said I would stay. But she wouldn't have it. She would listen to it on the radio. They hugged her.

"Lay back down," she told Gid.

They gave us camouflage hunting coats that smelt like deer piss. And we piled in the cruiser and rode to the field. The parking lot was full of smoke. We pulled in a spot that was saved. The air smelt like charcoal and little sausages, and a recording of a marching band came raspy from the stadium speakers. Through the fence I could see the cheerleaders under the lights, hanging signs on the fence.

The Berry's tailgate was all older people just eating and shouting and backslapping. I thought it was very strange that no one was drinking. I could have taken a beer. John Frederick stood very close to me. If I took a step one way, he shuffled over.

Then a big bell started ringing and everyone formed two long walls through the parking lot. Then the players walked through, seniors first, wearing mustaches and elbow pads. They held hands and looked straight ahead. The grunts were at the back. They looked side to side, trying to slap every hand that reached from the crowd.

John Frederick pulled on my arm. I thought all the people were getting him spooked. But he was smiling. He shouted something about the Red Sea.

The deputy got us through the gate for free and we stood on the fence at the thirty-yard line. We watched the players doing jumping jacks and then the cheerleaders came out with big duffle bags and set them in front of us. I thought it lucky. They had paw prints on their cheeks.

By kickoff the stands were full and every foot of fence had a man leaning on it, and all wearing camouflage or caution orange. Lineville had a black kid at tailback who was fast as hell. He got free of a tackle in the backfield, hopped around the corner, and beat everybody down the sideline for an early score. Old man Berry tried to bring his fist down on the fence but missed. I began to wonder if he was strong enough to stand for four quarters. On the other side the band played something happy. On our side a man screamed that the Lineville line was holding. He told the ref to go to hell. The kicker missed the extra point.

The cheerleaders left their sweat suits and earmuffs on. They were just puffy things with ribbons in their hair and paint on their cheeks making a lot of noise. Maybe I did like them a little. Maybe I would have stood there without a coat just to see if the little one would cut her eyes at me a second time. I'm not saying I would do that now, not after all I found out about in Birmingham. But I would like to see John Frederick there again. The whole time he might as well have been standing out in his field, leaning on a hoe handle, watching a bunch of sixteen-year-old girls toss each other around. I figure rich people must look the same way at expensive paintings that they don't quite understand.

Ashland went ahead in the second half. Just before the game ended, the city police lined the field. But there wasn't any fighting that I could see.

When we got home we had to help old Berry up the steps.

"We done it again, Ma," he said. "They haven't beat us in the 2000s."

"Your daddy's asleep upstairs," she said to me. "He don't have a fever. I'll check on him tonight but I suspect he'll be fine tomorrow."

I thanked her.

"Mr. White, how did you like the game?"

"Oh yeah," he said. "I liked it good. I count twenty-two things I neber seen before."

I found Gid sitting against the headboard in the dark.

"Junior," he said. "Come sit for a minute."

I got on the end of the bed and kicked my shoes off. My toes were numb.

"It's a long day on a couch," he said.

"But it's not cold."

"How cold is it?"

"Feel my hands," I said, and reached for his face.

"No, Junior. We'll go when it warms up. What? I don't know where."

"I didn't say nothing."

"I have started thinking about it."

"Yeah?"

"I thought about it all day. Starting over somewhere. Maybe all three of us getting a little business of some kind. Something good and honest. Building swing sets maybe. Shit if I know. Gazebos or something."

"That'd be fine."

"I know it would. But then I remember we ain't got any money. And no one would give me a business license, 'cause the state's got my name on file. And yours too probably. I'm thinking too much. I keep remembering the thing I done and how maybe it wasn't all right. Could be I was part to blame for her acting out. Maybe I did-n't know how to take care of her and that's why she run off and do all that. What I mean is, maybe I drove her to fool with that boy. I didn't even close my eyes when I let it go. I just looked right at him and he was laying under her looking at me and I meant to get her next but I just put the pistol on the roof of the car I bought her and I drove away. That boy had it coming, but it weren't his family's fault. He had two boys and a little girl. JoBell told me. And I think about them some, his kids. They're probably fine people, just stuck with a bad one like I was stuck with her."

"They'll be all right."

"I don't know. I go thinking too long and I can't keep from asking what's the reason all this is happening. And I think of sixty-one years and all I ever done is hurt people by accident. Like this woman who couldn't go to the game tonight. I don't know what I'm saying except that I don't know if it's worth trying to make it all a little better. That's all I ever done and look where I got."

"That's all anyone does," I said.

"Does what?"

"Tries to make it a little better."

"You're right. They're fixing up their house so they can feel better. Cleaning out their gutters and building outdoor garages. And they're doing all their jobs so they can get a little more money and feel a little safer. But it never works. They get a little more and then they go back to feeling the way they did before they had it."

He had it going pretty fast.

"When you're young, Junior, you work hard so your momma will say 'good job.' Then you do it for a gal, and maybe it works and you get one. And maybe she's all you ever really wanted and it's good for a year or more, but then you stop trying to prove anything to her and you start trying to win your own self. But you can't ever do that, Junior. You can tell yourself you're doing good all the time but you'll never believe it. You can set a goal and get it, then not remember that you set it. And you'll always wonder if you're full of shit and have never meant one thing you've ever said. To your own self or anybody else either. And you can't ever know. It's like we all got jury out in another room, and we're waiting and waiting, but they're never coming back."

I took one of his pillows and lay it on the footboard. I pulled the sheets out and slid my legs under.

19.

"Your friend said something sweet this morning," the mother said. "He stood up from the table and put his hand up like this and he said, 'You know, there's only three people in this world. There's Jesus, and there's Satan, and there's Merit White.'"

"I heard him say it too," Samuel said. He came in the kitchen wearing an old Auburn sweater and he held onto the counter to rest. "The man says some strange things."

"I thought it was nice," his wife said.

"Where is he?" I said.

"Sammy took him out cruising. They're making the rounds. He was so happy when Sammy asked him."

Gid was on the sofa with the sports page. He was acting weak and tired, but he couldn't keep his foot from tapping.

"You're up, Junior," he said. "Come, let's chop some wood. We'll build these good people a fire. You chop and I'll stack."

Outside, Gid got going about John Frederick. Saying why would he go cruising with the deputy, and he bet he would spill the truth. The wood was good and dry, and I made short, measured swings, trying not to listen.

———

We were watching the pregame show when we heard the dogs running down the front steps and the slam of car doors. John Frederick came in with the deputy. He stood behind the couch with his hands in his pockets and his shoulders rolled over like dough. Gid noticed him during a commercial and said, "Take a seat, old man. Tell us how many criminals you hauled in this morning."

But he shuffled out and went upstairs. I went to look after him. The door to the room was cracked. He was talking to the wall.

"Oh yes. That is true. Some are for womens and some are for God. But there be another kind too. 'Cause some are for both. You can sing the good ones about God or a girl. Whicheber you want."

I stuck my head around again. He was sitting on the bed and I remembered the night when everything had changed. I had done the same thing—peeked and pulled back. And I stood there in the hall listening. I imagined that, to him, nothing had changed too much. There he was with his knees to the wall.

"Here's one you might know already. You might hab sang it in church without knowing it be about a lady too. Hah. You ready?"

He sang low and long. I snuck in and sat on the other bed.

Don't leabe me by and by,
I am laden bad tonight,
Don't leabe me by and by,
Won't you stay inside, won't you stay inside.

After a while he got up and sang to the window. His voice wasn't much more than a whisper, though it had power enough. He was stopping sharp at the end of every line, like he was whipping himself with the words. Then he turned around. He smiled a little.

"There you be," he said. "I thought an angel was singing with me. Could hab been an angel and you."

He said he was tired from all that riding, that he'd never gone so far in one day, and that the deputy said the woods were full of drugs.

I told him there was soup downstairs.

I went back to watching the game. At halftime he still hadn't come down. So I fixed a bowl and took it up. I set it on the table beside the bed. He didn't wake up.

During the second half the phone rang. The deputy answered in the kitchen and he talked soft. It was a short call. Then he came in the room and stood very still. I didn't look at him. I just thought, *it is over now. And I should have told Gid he didn't kill that man. He could have turned himself in and spared some embarrassment.*

"What is it, hon?" his momma asked.

The deputy was behind me. He drew a few breaths without letting anything out. I didn't look. I just watched his parents. Mr. Berry started nodding.

"He got the call," he said.

"What call?" the woman asked. She smoothed her apron across her lap. Then she knew. She stood up. "Iraq?"

"Yeah, Momma."

His parents followed him into the kitchen. I thought I could be sick.

Gid didn't pay attention to any of it. Auburn was losing bad, and before it was over, he went upstairs. I watched till the end, saw the Georgia players dance around the field, then turned the TV off. I heard the family in the kitchen.

"You'll come home for Christmas?" she asked.

"Yeah. After training. Then I'll ship out."

"Will they let me send you jelly?"

"I think so."

I tried to sneak past the kitchen to go upstairs, but Mrs. Berry called after me.

"You'll come to church with us in the morning, won't you, Merit?"

I said I would. Then I went upstairs and found Gid.

"I got to get out, go for a walk, find me a beer, something," he said. "I hate being cooped up. It's too damn familiar."

I sat in the chair in the corner.

"Them people down there are nice to have us. But damn if I can sit on a couch for another minute. And don't you think they're a little off? A little too happy and perfect?"

I shrugged.

"And you notice they ain't asking anymore if I need to borrow the phone? But they're too shy to ask us to leave. And I believe that woman would adopt you."

He went to the window.

"I don't know, Junior. Maybe I'm the one off. But I'll tell you one thing I do know: Our khaki-pant-wearing coach should work for the Army. All he's good for is recruiting."

He drew on the glass where his breath had fogged. He couldn't calm down.

It didn't make any difference to John Frederick that we had woken him to go walking around in the night. He asked no questions, and when we were out on the highway, frozen in the moonlight, he walked out in front of us with that blanket cloaking him like he was some kind of priest.

We wore stolen coats that were good and warm. I stayed out on the yellow line. Thin clouds blew across the moon and their shadows crossed the street. I lagged back a little, kicked a pinecone out in front of me, and hoped the Berrys wouldn't worry too much about the note we left. I had told Gid not to heap it on so heavy, but he had. Anyway, we were out of there. Gid said all the pleasantry was making him itch, that being around people that trusting can make a man feel dangerous."

20.

WE NEVER TALKED ABOUT WHICH WAY WE WOULD GO. IF ANOTHER ROAD looked nicer, one of us would take it and we'd go that way. The only rule was try not to go back the way we had come. Try not to make any circles. You can get lucky anyplace once.

One night John Frederick looked down in a ditch and saw a deer dying. Maybe a truck had hit it. The thing was hoofing at the air. Gid kept on, pretending not to see. The old man looked pleasantly at the animal. I had to pull him away.

"In heaben it will be light all day," he said, and he got my arm. "There be no night there and peoples will be able to see the deers before they hit them. How 'bout that? Streets made of gold and no animals dead on the side."

I got to wondering why he wanted to live so long if he thought heaven was so suited for him. But I didn't ask him. I was tired of him telling about it. Instead I imagined a smashed rattlesnake on gold pavement. That was the only good thing about winter—you could walk through the woods without watching where you stepped. Spring seemed so far away then. My ears stung in the cold, and knew that I should tell Gid and end it.

He was a ways ahead, walking squatty and sure. I hurried to catch him, to tell him that he had closed his eyes and the gun had moved and the bullet had glanced the guy's skull and gone into the

backseat of Robyn's Sunbird, the one he half-bought her on her for-
tieth birthday with a personalized license plate that she made him
remove. Then he could just take his sentence and know that he'd
still have some time on the other end to sit around and make stuff
and watch the Braves. It would shame him some to know that he
hadn't handled the weapon well. But hell, he was used to shame.

I caught up with him and put my hand on his shoulder.

"Look," he said, and pointed across the field.

"The freeway."

"Good, Junior. But look a little higher. It's the Waffle House."

I scratched my ribs through my jacket and thought about scattered hash browns and butter floating on a bowl of grits. And I waited for the old man to catch up.

———

I had John Frederick by the arm as we came through the parking lot, and we saw Gid through the window. He had a table and he
was smoking a cigarette the waitress had given him. Two cops were
at the other end of the place, smoking at the low bar. At the high bar
in the middle were two men in silk vests and top hats. There were
five or six plates of food before them, and while I got John Frederick
in the booth they stared at us and said things with their mouths full.

"Here. Figure out what you want," Gid said. He was a bad smok-
er. He put it too far in his mouth and looked at the ash as he pulled.
Then took some menus from behind the ketchup. "Take your coat off,
Junior. Ma'am. Pardon me, ma'am. Could you pour these gentlemen
two cups of your freshest coffee? We might be ready to order too."

The girl set two mugs in front of us and slid the cream and
sugar over. She smiled nicely and went down the bar, and I watched
the place where her apron was knotted. I leaned over the booth and
looked at her ankles. She wore pantyhose and those sneakers old
women wear, the medical kind that always look like they have begun

to deflate. There was a waffle crust on the tile. She spied it and bent to get it. As she was standing up, a piece of toast landed there. One of the gentlemen in the silk had tossed it. The police looked at him. He took a link of sausage, dripping with syrup, and stuffed it in his mouth. And he stared at the girl while she stooped for the toast. Then she was by our table.

"Do you want one of my cigarettes too?" she said. I looked at her. "They're Winstons."

"I'm all right."

"I should quit too," she said. "I don't do it around my little girl though."

"Just cut it back a little," Gid said.

She walked down the bar and talked to the other waitress. They stood behind the cook and looked at us and whispered. The cook paid no attention. He had tattoos up his wrists, and when he had dumped the bacon on the plates, he wiped his hands on his towel and walked through the swinging door into the back.

Our girl brought us water and asked us what we wanted.

"I'll take three eggs extra easy," Gid said, "with the grits and the toast and a double side of the hash browns, scattered and cooked to hell. Junior here will take the same, but with two eggs. And bacon with that. Old man? You know what you'll have."

John Frederick told her his name. She shook his hand and helped him order. Gid put his cigarette out. He dabbed it a bunch of times, pinched it, and folded it in half.

The girl hung our order above the grill. The men at the high bar stared at her as she moved back and forth. They chewed and called after her, but she ignored them.

"Those policemen looking at us?" Gid asked.

"No."

"Don't look at them."

"I'm not."

"You just did."

I finished my water.

"I thought of something on the way over here," he said. He leaned over the table and spoke quiet. "I was thinking that we could go over to Mississippi and take the old man here and set him up with some of those boys that do the recordings of all the old blues men. They could make a gospel record of him and you could be his manager."

I took a little more cream.

"I'm not fooling," he said.

I nodded and had some coffee.

"Well, don't tell me what you think of it," he said.

"Okay."

He got squinty and pointed his spoon at me.

"Junior," he said. "You're too young to be like that."

"You spit in my coffee," I said.

He switched it with his.

"What about you?" I asked.

"How do you mean?"

"If we get him set up, what do we do with you?"

"I think we could fake my death."

I laughed at him. "How do you want to die?"

"Suicide. You could tell them I got tired of running and I went up on the bridge and jumped down in the Alabama River."

The girl came over. She asked us what we were up to on a night like that. Out so late in the middle of the week. We ignored her.

"You want to be a gospel singer old man?" Gid asked.

John Frederick blushed.

"We'll get you a new suit with a necktie and a belt with a shiny buckle. Would you like that?"

Our food came then and we dropped it. Gid didn't thank her and John Frederick didn't pray. I unwrapped some butter and pushed it in my grits. It was hot next to John Frederick. He hadn't taken the blanket off his shoulders.

I got to thinking about his trailer. I imagined a family of raccoons had come through the window and laid a litter of babies on the couch. Or that some cousin had decided he had disappeared, as his wife had, and had taken the place for himself. Or maybe a tornado had finally smashed it, and if you went walking through the woods, the trees would have the insulation dangling like cotton candy. Then I wasn't sure if his place even had insulation. I was still wondering as I cleaned my plate with some toast. And I realized that I had eaten everything without tasting any of it. On my hash brown plate was some ketchup and oil. I rubbed the crust through it.

Gid went to the bathroom. The old man put his hand on mine.

"They're not gonna take your daddy to the prison tonight," he said. "And when it's time, they won't shoot him."

He broke some crackers over his chili and stirred them through.

"That's good," I said. Until then, I wasn't sure if he even knew why we'd been wandering. "Good," I said.

"That's right. My cousin, the one who makes the blues on the guitar, she shoot her man because she tired of him beating on her. And the police knew she was not a mean woman, though she mean enough when she find a bottle, but not so mean to kill a person just for the killing. And your daddy not either. They'll just put him under the prison. And I bet we even see him going down the road some days picking trash off the grass."

I noticed our girl down the counter. She was face-to-face with the coffeemaker, painting her eyes up in the aluminum reflection. The fancy gentlemen were pointing at her butt. The other girl walked by and pinched it. She jumped.

John Frederick went on. "He knows what he want to be, but he's not that. And now he scared that the prison will keep him from eber being something. Scared that he neber will be. You know whateber you scared of the most is the thing you lub the most. If you scared that your child gonna die, then you lub your child the most. Some are scared that they gonna lose their jobs. They lub money the most. Your daddy, he lubs manhood. But me, I lub God the most. God,

Jesus, and the Ghost. And the only thing that can make me shake and holler is if God said he didn't want me anymore. Yes sir. But I know it can't happen because he already did that one time. He said I don't want you, Jesus. I don't want you. And he turned his head away so he could look at me. That's why I don't get scared eber. I lub him most, but I know he won't go away from me."

Gid came back. Our girl had cleared the table except for our mugs. She filled them and gave us more cream. Then she went down the bar and gave the cops some change. The younger one went to the jukebox and put on some Lynyrd Skynyrd.

I poured some cream in my coffee and watched the color turn. It made me think of a muddy river in summer. Of swinging naked from a vine and the moment when you let go. Of pulling your knees up so your heels don't bruise on the bottom. Then looking at the tree roots before you climb out, making sure there aren't any snakes knotted. *Sweet Home Alabama.* I guess so.

I was considering what it would be like to sleep under the interstate when our check was handed to us. Gid stared at me. My coffee looked gray. I drank it and came up with a plan. We would ask to pay with a credit card. But they only take cash, so we would go around the corner to the Citgo and use the ATM. Then we would get away. I told it to Gid, the music hiding my voice.

"Check your pockets again," he said.

I didn't do it.

"Nothing left?"

"Same as yesterday."

"Then I guess that's the way. But it's always a little thing that gets you caught for the big one."

"It'll work," I said.

"Then you and the old man say good-bye and head for the car. Just go across the street and wait. I'll go to the can again and when I come out I'll ask to pay with a card."

"That's fine."

"I'm always having to do the shit," he said.

I put my hand on the old man's shoulder and woke him up. I was gonna tell him to scoot on out when the other waitress, a tall, orange-haired girl, stood by our table and said, "Candi likes you."

Our girl was standing by the grill. She hid behind the cook. He nudged her away and she stood with her little back to us. The orange girl whispered, "She wants you to ask her out."

"That'd be fun," I said.

Candi gathered herself. She walked down the bar and went through the swinging door. But she came right back out following a big woman who we hadn't seen before. She tore a page off her pad and put it on the table. It said, "Candi 435-4065."

"You can call me," she said. She took our check and looked down at the fat woman. "It's time for the shift change," she whispered. "I told her y'all had paid up."

I realized then that she had taken her apron off. She walked back through the door. The orange-girl had been watching beside the cook. She came to our table then.

"You better call her," she said. "She's good."

We went outside, circled behind a gas station, and walked into the woods. We went along the interstate, just inside the trees. Soon we came to an old wire fence, but we didn't try to get over. We just spread the blankets there and lay down.

I kept thinking about how we had gotten out of there. I wanted to laugh about it, and the coffee kept me awake for a long time. I tried to find her number, just to look at it. Girls' handwriting has always meant something to me. I reached down one pocket and down the other. But it wasn't there. My throat got tight. I had left it on the table. The damn girl, I thought. She will see it there and put it in the trash with everything else. And she will go home and wash her eyes and smoke while her little girl sleeps. Damn me. I listened to the freeway and watched the sky brighten through the twigs. A few leaves were still holding on, waving.

21.

NORTH HAD BEEN THE WAY. OUR ROUTE HAD BEEN WINDY ENOUGH, BUT always, we had been drifting up. It may have been the coming cold, or maybe Gid still had Mississippi in mind, but we turned hard to the west without a word about it. And then there was no more ambling, no more standing at a crossroads until someone picked a way.

Gid was always checking the shoulders for half-smoked cigarettes. He'd do pretty well when we'd pass a church. Then he'd light one and go to bragging.

"When I was your age, I was mean and full of piss," he said. "My friends, we went out one night and got the idea to dig up Franny Blankenship's grave. She was part Indian and she married the man who was the first mayor of Columbus. They said she was buried with black pearls around her neck. So we got up some shovels and picks and beer and we drove to the back side of the Liberty church and got drunk in the parking lot."

He pulled again at his cigarette but it had gone out. We stopped while he lit it.

"I told you about it before?" he asked.

I told him he hadn't.

"Midnight came around and it was Sunday. Out there in the graveyard there was two damn monuments bigger than all the rest.

They're still there, I guess. One for Franny and one for her husband. We got to work when the beer was done and we were pretty drunk. So we're picking and shoveling in turns and about an hour later Buddy Conway pulls his pick up and he's put it right through her eyehole. Her head's laying there on the pick and Buddy's dropped it and we're all laid out on the ground. All but Ed Crum. He was the meanest and froze in Korea a year later trying to swim across a river to get to the boys in the tower that shot off his hand. So he jumps down in the hole and starts pawing for the pearls and finds them. We drove to Crum's place because his daddy always stayed late in Phenix City, gambling and grabbing after the hookers. We sat on his porch and we were sober as judges. None of us could talk but Crum. And he says, 'Listen here. Anybody tells anybody about this and I'll knock your block off. Y'all ain't but fifteen but I'm eighteen and they'll put me in the prison if they find out. Here's what we'll do. I counted and there's fifteen pearls. And there's seven of us. We'll all take two and we'll put the biggest one in a box in the corner block at the top of the old Stewart's millhouse. And every year, on this night, November something, we'll meet there and make the strand unbroken again.'

"The damn thing was that Buddy left his pick there by the grave when we run off. And right there on the handle was his daddy's name. Ernest Conway, I think. So in the morning the preacher gets there first and sees all the dirt dug up. And we all got drug out of bed by our daddies. All but Crum. Buddy Conway gave everyone's name but his, and none of us ever told. So we all took the heat and did about a thousand hours of community service. The paper wrote about it for a week. And no one ever knew Crum was there too until he dies in Korea and all of Phenix City is making him a hero. He was the halfback in high school too. Everybody loved him but they were scared of him too. He had failed three grades and he left after our freshman year for the war. So some officer told the newspaperman that Crum always wore these three black pearls alongside his dog tags and then everyone knew. It was better for us then because no one could look bad at us for doing the same as a hero had done."

We passed a lot of outlet malls with their long, empty parking lots, and behind them were some old iron mills, dark against the sky. Then some churches with the fake brick and the painted mortar lines, and a lot of small houses with wheelchair ramps.

"Where we now?" John Frederick said.

"This is Birmingham," Gid said.

We passed a motel that had free cable. We talked about trying to get a room but just kept on. We walked on into morning and climbed up under an interstate bridge. Gid started reading the graffiti, shouting against the noise overhead.

"Jesus saves," he shouted.

"That's right," John Frederick said.

"For a real good time call Sally."

"All right."

"Foreigners go home."

"Yeah. Come back home."

We woke up and headed for the middle of it all. Clouds blew low and the wind got a grocery bag and slapped it against some razor wire atop a fence. I tried to get my jacket closed up but the zipper caught. I jerked it up and down but it wouldn't move. We were downtown, but the big buildings weren't any help with the wind. It ran through the streets like a mob.

A man called to us from some church steps. He said give him some money because a snowstorm was coming and he needed a suite at the Tutweiler.

"Snow?" Gid said.

"Four to six," the man said, and he screwed the top back on his bottle. "Any minute, all night."

We were through the big buildings and John Frederick grabbed my arm.

"You want to lib in that city?" he said.

"No."

"I bet you don't. No. You need to be someplace quiet. Me too. When I sit on my plow tractor, I pull things out of my head to see what they look like. I look at them upside and ober to see if I got the right things in there or not. I bet you do the same thing when you go walking through the woods."

"I try not to think much."

"All right," he said, and then he went to coughing.

The bass line of some music was pumping somewhere. The road forked. We took the low prong that headed towards the music. Up above a streetlight there was an overpass. And off to the left of the little road was a bar with big trucks out front. It was a narrow little thing with a sign fanned across the roof like the top fin of a bluegill. The music came through the aluminum walls. Gid stopped in the street and looked at the place.

A few raindrops fell on the pavement. It was going to come then. We hurried for the overpass. The rain came heavy and the wind spit it under the bridge. We headed up the ramp. The wind swung under the bridge like a cat under a couch, and we sat in the only corner where it couldn't quite reach, me in the middle. We tucked the blanket under our legs.

"It'll turn to ice first," Gid said. "Then snow. It's just now cold enough."

"I hope it comes a foot," I said.

"We won't get a foot. But we should've gone south. Down through Eufala and Dothan. Hell, maybe even into Florida. The panhandle's a lot like Alabama if you think about it."

"So is Georgia and every other place."

"The hell it is."

I laughed at him.

"What's that cocky shit?"

"Nobody's any different from nobody else," I said.

"I'm not talking about people. I'm talking about the states they live in."

I shook my head.

"You ever walked across the bridge from Phenix City to Columbus?"

I didn't answer.

"Have you?"

"I can't remember."

"You have but you were too blind to notice. You can feel it in your head when you go down the other side. You can feel it like someone's pushing their fingers into your skull."

I smiled at the way he said it.

"I ain't lying," he said. "When all those boys got run out of town for the gambling and the girls, it weren't anything different than what was happening on the other side of the river. Not too much worse. Only the people on one side pointed their fingers while the others minded their own damn lives. That's the difference. We do shit in Alabama and we don't cover it up. We don't know how, maybe, or maybe we don't even try. But whatever it is, we ain't pointing our fingers and talking too quiet."

"What about Mississippi?" I said. "And your plan for him?"

"I was gonna tell you. Mississippi's got shit about it. But people ain't covering up there either. They don't put their fingers in anybody's soup. We could live there. And we could live in the panhandle. But nowhere else."

A minute later he said, "Don't talk about things you don't know nothing about."

The rain came steady. After a while Gid began to doze. He leaned over and curled behind my back so that I couldn't lie down. I pulled my arms inside my coat, and went to watching the sheets of rain blow across the spotlights on top of the bar. They moved like minnow schools.

PART TWO

1.

Don't nobody really live in Birmingham. Some work there, some look for work, but they all stay on any of a hundred hills that they have given other names. I have heard that if two people from Birmingham meet, one won't ask the other "Where do you live?" but, "Where are you from?" And the other will say Hoover, Trussville, Irondale, Vestavia, or someplace else you could drive in five minutes. So it wasn't Birmingham where a woman laid her leg across mine and told me she liked to hear me talk. That's not where she taught me about dreaming—that rich name for discontent. It was in Mountain Brook, maybe two miles from the bridge where we had ducked from a storm, where, when the wind blew a certain way, we could hear the music coming from a Birmingham bar.

Gid was in there when I woke. John Frederick was either sleep-talking or praying. I doubled the blanket over his legs and went for the bar. In the gravel out front were a few dozen trucks, intimidating things with winches and mud tires and custom paint, and some of them diesel duellys. The rain pelted them as I ducked their mirrors and went to the door. There was no one there to ask my age. Gid was at the bar, on a barstool. I pulled one over, wiped some water from my hair, and looked around. On one side were a couple of pool tables under hanging lightbulbs. At the other end a woman sat on the stage with a cigarette. There was a crowd of guys in khaki pants talking to a few girls who looked all right. Looking at everyone, I remembered the trucks out front. It didn't make sense.

"Are we gonna sneak some beer in my coat?" I said.

"Fold your arms," Gid said. "And don't look that woman in the eye. Look at her throat or across the top of her hair."

The bartender came down and put a napkin in front of me.

"We'll take a hotty toddy," Gid told her. "Them beers made me colder."

"We don't serve hot drinks," she said. "No stove."

"Don't y'all got a damn microwave or something back there?"

She nodded and looked at me. Then she gathered the foil Gid had shredded from his bottle.

"A microwave'll work," he said. "Just drop some whiskey in a coffee mug and heat it for a minute. Bring me some honey and one of your lemons and I'll do the rest."

The bar girl smirked then. But she took a bottle from the shelf and slipped past a curtain.

"Junior, I'm still shivering," he said. "And what about the old man out there? He should quit that preaching and come in for a coffee."

"He's fine," I said.

"You hear him coughing?"

"I heard him."

"Jesus drank."

"Are we gonna stuff these drinks in my coat?"

The girl came through the curtain, careful to keep the mugs level. She had a honey bear under her elbow. She sat it all down and pulled a spoon from the back pocket of her jeans. Then she walked down the bar to help another guy.

"Look how much she gave us," Gid said. "But she forgot the lemons."

She came back as he was reaching over the bar for the tray of cocktail fruits.

"Thank you ma'am," Gid said. "And thanks for the soldier's portions. You're a nice lady."

Gid squeezed some honey in our drinks and squirted the lemons. He licked his fingers and said that it was a good bar we had found. You could tell, he said, because everybody was minding their own business. There was a mirror behind the bottles, and through the bottles were strands of Christmas lights. They were blue and white, and they reminded me of winter.

Gid took a few swallows and got going about his wife. He said that if he missed her some it was only because he had forgotten how it was. He said he was always thinking about year one and forgetting the other thirteen. That's how a mind is, he had learned, always trying to trick its own self. So sure, we were out in a winter rain and it would be easy to picture her at twenty-nine in a yellow bikini, but he wouldn't do it. He said he'd take all the snow in Buffalo before he lived with another woman who pretended he wasn't there.

He kept on about it, but I barely listened. Instead I noticed how nice and square the bar girl's shoulders looked under her sweater, and how, when she walked down the bar, the back of her legs were like a pair of seesaw planks.

"Why don't you put a little of that to your lips," Gid said. "It'll stop your shaking."

She was standing down the bar and she was looking at us. I lifted the cup to my mouth but the steam rushed my nose and burnt my lungs. I pulled back quick and set the mug down hard so that the drink rocked and some spilt over. Gid hit me on the back. It made me cough.

"In a couple of months we'll not need it hot," he said. "I've been thinking about that a lot. The spring. Maybe if things work out, we'll stop all this and start something new."

I looked at him.

"I had a boat once," he said. "Before you came around. I made fort-two thousand a year and was only twenty-seven votes short of the county commission. I'd walk through the mall with my wife and watch the boys turn green as money. I had all them things, but I didn't feel right. And then, when I decided on a simple life, when I tried to peel everything away and get to the pure pleasures, and when I decided that every friend I had wouldn't take a rubber bullet to save me and they could all go to hell in a Cadillac, it weren't enough to make a clean break. I just replaced one thing for another. Same as me trying for nine years to get people to call me an artist. And they did finally. I never told you all the pretty things people would say. But it only got me hollow even more and I had to act out. But sometimes lately, just here lately when us three are walking and the preacher's singing those songs, I feel all right. I feel good. When it's like that, and there's not any damn rain or chill, I don't think about nothing. Now drink some more of your juice."

"It's cheap stuff," I said.

"And how would you know better? You want her to put a little water in it?"

"Why is she staring at us?"

"That woman, Junior, is staring at me."

"Is she?"

"That's right. Has been since I made an entrance. And don't look at me that way. You see the other ones in here. They're all boys with their mother's cheeks. But that woman is tired of boys. Girls grow up faster."

He said it very serious, and I laughed at him.

"I mean that," he said.

"I know you do."

"You know I do?"

I looked down the bar to where a veiny-armed woman was waving her cigarette and talking to nobody. Then I checked on the bar girl.

"I don't know where it was Junior, but somewhere along the way you started knowing every damn thing."

"I don't know why she's watching us."

"That's because you don't listen. I just told you why. And stop looking down there. She probably wants to ask you for some ID."

I took another drink. It tasted like medicine.

Gid got up and looked for the bathroom. The boys by the pool tables let him through. They grinned as he passed. One pretended to hook his thumbs in some imaginary overall straps.

The girl closed the register and put some guy's change on the counter. He pushed it back at her. She walked towards me. I fingered the handle of my mug. Then she was standing there. I thought she might do some chore but she was very still. So I looked over my shoulder to see if someone was waiting to order. There was no one. I thought she wanted me to pay for our drinks. I tried to make up a plan but I couldn't think. She folded her arms and her sweater came up a little. I could see her hip bone.

"Don't you want to take your coat off?" she said.

I pulled on the zipper to show her it was broken.

"Oh," she said, and she went to help another guy.

My pants were a little wet and my seat started to itch. I scooted around on the stool. Gid was taking a long time. Someone racked the pool balls and someone else cracked them. The girl came back, stood there. I kept sliding around on my seat.

"Are you hungry?" she said.

I didn't understand.

"Have you had anything to eat tonight?"

I looked towards the bathroom for a minute.

"We just ate," I said, and I took a drink.

"What'd you have?"

"Supper."

"How was it?"

She was asking too fast. I shrugged.

"You can't pull your coat over your head?"

I looked her in the face. In one eye, then in the other, back and forth. She bowed her head and twisted a towel in her hands. I looked

to the pool tables, where, in the yellow light, two guys were compar-
ing their stomach muscles. They had their polo shirts pulled up for
a girl to punch. She hit one and grabbed her hand. She didn't know
how to make a fist. The guy hugged her. I watched the whole thing
play out, thinking that the bar girl would walk away. But now she
was looking at me again. I had a drink.

She leaned over the counter. Her mouth was by my ear.

"I know who you are."

I set my mug down. "No. I've never been here."

She was just standing there, and I kept sipping. She took a pen
from her pocket and wrote on a napkin. She spun it for me.

"Merit?" it said. And she said it quiet. "Merit."

I slid my drink handle from one hand to the other. I had an idea
to sling it in her eyes. She was just standing there. Finally she went
down the bar. I pushed back from it and slid off my seat. The boys
weren't quick to let me through. So I went around the table. I was
about to bang on the bathroom door when she took my wrist. She
tugged me into a corner.

"Are you okay?" she said. "Do you know where you're going?"

"We're not going anywhere."

"Nowhere?"

"What do you want?"

"I want to get you something to eat."

"No ma'am," I said. "We got to be leaving."

"You do," she said. "Okay." She thumbed some hair from her
eyes and bit her bottom lip. But she held her eyes against me. She
said, "Is the old man still with you?"

I stood a little straighter. Damn her.

"He's seventy-four," I said.

"Where is he?"

I nodded towards the bridge. Gid walked by and didn't see us in
the shadow. I watched him looking at my stool. He glanced in my
mug, then switched it with his.

"I'm sorry," she said. "I'm not really like this. I'm Haley."

I shrugged.

"It's an awful night to be outside."

"No. It's not bad."

"I could give you a place to stay for a few nights."

"Why?"

"Does it matter why, really? Does it? Listen, I have to work. But if you want, you could get your friend and bring him around back. He could at least warm up in the kitchen for a little while."

"No," I said. "He doesn't drink."

Around the pool table I saw a lot of people looking our way. They were laughing—they thought I was in trouble, stole something, maybe—and I imagined it would be satisfying to take a knife across their turtlenecks. For a minute I saw it all go down. They'd get their golf clubs out of their toolboxes and that would be it. Then something happened. Against all the other faces, all tall and easy, hers was suddenly decent. Besides, I would have had to push her to get by. "That'd be all right," I said. "I'll bring him around."

"And I'll keep your dad happy."

"His name's Gid."

She nodded like she already knew. Then she stepped out of my way. I brushed past some people and walked out in the rain. When I crossed the street, I heard John Frederick singing. I stood behind a concrete pylon and listened.

Got a big girl, she watch me plow
She watch me plow all day.
Got a big girl, she watch me bail
She watch me bail the hay.
The plowing's for the children
For them a piece to eat.
And the bailing's for my big girl
In the hay I lub her sweet.

Then I walked up into the shadows.

"Oh, okay," he said. "You come back, yeah. Yes you did. But our friend still having him a stiff drink."

I helped him up and gathered our stuff. John Frederick went to gazing at the rain in a streetlight. I let him watch it for a while. Then I took his arm and walked him down the bank.

Out from the cover the rain beaded on his hat and dangled on his beard. I led him across the street and around the puddles in the gullied parking lot. When we were going around back, a cat stopped in the light and looked at us. The light shone through the small barred window of the back door. I opened it without knocking.

2.

THERE IS SOMETHING ABOUT WIND MOVING THROUGH BROKEN GLASS. They are the same thing, the wind and the shards, and together they make a sound that hovers over your skin like a knife. I turn the television up so I cannot hear it. Auburn will play Alabama, and the announcers are shouting their predictions. It is a giant TV, and there are speakers all around. They are between the books and family photographs and in the corners of the crown molding, and they talk at me from every side. But I can watch my hairs move around on my arm, combed by the sound I cannot hear.

I do not remember if I trusted her at the beginning. It seems a long way back. But I remember my elbows chattering against my ribs, and the whiskey in my nose, and then her hip bones behind the bar, and the sound of my name.

In the kitchen were a long sink and a short Mexican. He dipped the glasses in the water and set them on a rack. The music was going loud and he didn't hear us when I opened the door. I went in first and gave the old man a hand up. The door had laid open against the outside wall. I had to hop down to pull it shut. The man washing dishes saw us then. He wiped his hands and went quickly through the curtain. The girl came in holding someone's credit card. She said something to the man in Spanish, something about us. Then he followed her into the bar. There was a coffeemaker working on the table. The little man came in and sat some chairs out. Then he went back to work.

John Frederick coughed hard into his sleeve.

"Wooo. Yes sir," he said. "I swallow a june bug when I was seventy-one. And sometimes he crawls back up my pipe and buzzes in my throat. I used to hope I cough him out."

I made myself a cup of coffee in a beer mug and poured some milk for the old man. And together we sat and watched her sneakers underneath the curtain.

"She is a sight," he said.

"She knows about Gid."

"Your daddy?"

"Yeah."

"She knows he's a drinker?"

I smiled at him.

"Oh yeah," he said. "I bet she saw him in there. You might neber hab heard this before. But if Jesus comes back tonight, riding down the sky, all of those people in there are gonna see two Jesuses. They can't tell which one to worship."

He got up and stood by the man at the sink.

"You put those cups in and out the water like a drunk man's face. That's right. But those people out there need to be baptized because even if you're sober, you don't know all about it."

The guy scooted over a little bit. He was a foot shorter. John Frederick shuffled closer to him and watched him work. Then he started handing him the dirty mugs. It didn't speed the job. But it helped the man relax.

The girl came back through the curtain and pointed to the old man. She liked him.

"You a little warmer?" she said.

"Thanks."

"We're gonna switch Gid to coffee. He won't talk to me." She fixed one, then said, "If y'all would like to, you can sit in my car. I'll give you my keys. You could lay back the seats and sleep."

"We're okay."

"Well, if you change your mind, I'll set them here. It's the green one out back. And I ordered a pizza for you."

She brought it in a few minutes later. I told John Frederick to come eat. I spread the box across our laps and started into it. I ate the crust of a few pieces while the rest of it cooled.

Her keys were there on the counter. There was a wallet attached. I slid the box onto the old man's lap and got up. I undid the Velcro on the wallet and saw her driver's license. It said:

Haley L. Snow

1450 Brookside Drive, Birmingham, AL.

I looked at her picture, then closed the thing quick, and sat back down. And I watched her feet moving under the curtain.

"A lot of people getting good and drunk," John Frederick said. "They gonna do some things they won't want to remember on the last day. They forgiben, but they still gonna hab to hear about it. In heaben they might be, but they won't hab the best jobs. Me, I want to be a gardener. I'd dig up earth that doesn't weigh anything. No rocks either. And sometimes I'll sit right down in the earth and eat from the bine. And when I get up, there won't be any dirt on my britches. That's how it be there. Dark dirt that won't get you dirty. Yeah."

He stared up at the ceiling. I decided that it was his first time in a bar. He couldn't get over it. He wanted badly for time to end, for some burning chariot to carry him away. The door opened behind me and I jumped.

"Easy Junior," Gid said. He rocked back, then threw his foot up. "It ain't any warmer out there."

I let him have my seat. He took a slice.

"Kind of that woman to look out for us," he said.

I sat up on the table beside her keys and wondered if her car had a lot of gas in it. Gid looked at John Frederick, who was falling asleep. He pointed to the sauce on the old man's shirt.

"How 'bout that?" Gid said.

I shrugged.

"Got it all up and down."

He ate one piece and dropped the box on the floor. "It's gonna be a little harder for us to move around now. They put our pictures on the TV and across the top of the paper. But I've started figuring a way out."

He burped, and from across the kitchen, I smelt whiskey. Then he pointed to the man washing dishes.

"English?" he said.

I shrugged.

"I'll tell you about it when I get it all straightened out," he said. "I got to get it straight, and then I'll tell you."

He passed out pretty soon. I took the pizza box and set it on the counter beside the keys. The Mexican finished the dishes and got the girl to give him a beer. He sat down on the counter and talked on a cell phone.

I slid the keys against my leg and rubbed the leather wallet. I had an idea to pile the others in and drive off. But if it was a stick shift I couldn't do it. I'd never learned. I thought of going out to take a look but instead I just watched them sleep, stared into their open mouths. I thought I should get another chair and squeeze in between them, for habit's sake.

I pushed the keys away and went to the door. The rain had almost stopped. I saw the cat come out from under her car. It ran around a puddle and under a bush.

"Merit," she said. I turned around. "You can sit out here if you want. I'm just cleaning up. There's no one left."

I followed her through the curtain and climbed in the same seat I had before. She gave me a beer.

"You got enough to eat?" she said.

"Yeah. We'll be out of here soon."

She wiped the counter. Then she took the jugs and emptied the tip money into a big envelope. She did chores behind my end of the bar. She took the spouts out of the bottles and gave them to the little man. And she gave him all the ashtrays. The whole time the guy was on his cell phone.

The girl peeked through the curtain.

"They're both snoring," she said. "Do they do that every night?"

"I don't know."

"I told Gid that y'all can stay at my house. My parents are out of town for a while and there's plenty of room."

She said good night to the Mexican and locked the door behind him. And she poured herself a glass of wine and sat beside me.

"Are your feet sore?" she asked.

"I've been sitting down all night."

She took the napkin from under her glass. She pushed the edges down and spun it by the corners for a while. Then she pulled a piece of hair from behind her ear, looked at it, and put it back.

"It freaked me out when you came in here," she said. "I had this feeling all day that I would see you somewhere. I told Gid. The newspaper ran a story this morning about y'all. And the TV news picked it up tonight. Anyway, I'm sorry I was so aggressive."

I looked at the Christmas lights strung blue and white behind the bottles, and I thought of police cars.

"Gid told me that you're headed for Mississippi," she said.

"He's drunk."

"I'm sorry."

The music was off and the place was quiet. It was the kind of joint you'd find in our county, and I wondered again why all those rich kids came there. I finished my beer quick.

Then she said, "This girl was in tonight who tries to sell crank to all these rich kids. She kept leaning on the pool table and knocking the balls around. All the kids are scared of her, and she probably only weighs ninety pounds. It was funny. But sad too, you know?

She's stayed with me a few nights, but most of the time when I ask her she says no."

I looked at her then.

"Listen," I said. "A lot of people helped us out so far. It's been nice of everybody, and it's nice of you, but it ain't helping us figure anything out."

She took a swallow of wine.

"We'll stay with you tonight," I said. "But I don't want you to take good care of us. Not me or Gid. John Frederick don't matter. But don't let us stay another night. And don't let Gid get drunk anymore."

———

I sat in the front seat on the way to her house. The wiper blades swung slowly across the windshield. We had circled around the bar and driven across the overpass where we had been hiding out. We got off at the Mountain Brook exit. There were shops there and some stoplights. After the town were driveways that had little lights beside them. The trees in the yards had lights too, and the mist blew through the bare branches, and the trunks were black with rain. She took the bends easy, with her elbow on the door and her head in her hand. In the backseat the others were asleep.

"They're worn down?" she said.

I looked at them. Their heads were tilted towards the center, as if for a picture.

She let the radio play just above a whisper. And she talked just above that. She began a tour. This is where I went to school. This is where my dad plays golf. Back there, through that yard, is a magnolia tree I used to hide in. There's a pool behind that house where a lady drowned a litter of kittens then drowned herself. That's where Bull Connor lived. I know his grandson. He's all right.

We had climbed a hill and come into a fog.

"You can usually see the city from up here," she said. "The

buildings and all the rough neighborhoods. They look good at night. Like nothing's wrong down there. It bugs me how all of us up here come to see how pretty the city looks. Kids come up here to stare at poverty and make out. You tired?"

"No."

"We should get them in some beds," she said.

"Where are your parents?"

"They went skiing in Canada. They come back Saturday morning."

The house was made mostly of stone, and beside the arched wooden door two gas lamps burned. The drive led around the side of the house to a garage that looked like another house. We parked outside. She cut the motor.

I got out and opened John Frederick's door. His fly had busted and I saw his shirt through the gap. I put my hand on his shoulder and helped him out. And we followed her through a gate where copper-hatted lights lit the path to the back door.

3.

SHE FOLDED THE NEWSPAPER ON THE KITCHEN COUNTER AND PUT IT under a stack of mail. Then she put some water on the stove. She had shown the others to bed. We stood alone on the tile where lights shone from under the cabinets. I went to the refrigerator and looked at the pictures. There was one of her in some guy's arms on the beach. She wore a white dress. The guy was sunburned and a little fat. She came over. I stared down the holes in her jeans.

"That's my brother," she said, and pointed to the one I'd been looking at. "His name's Morgan. He goes to Alabama. I mean, he's not taking classes, but he lives in Tuscaloosa."

All of the people in all of the pictures looked pretty. Even the old people looked nice. She went to the door and kicked her shoes off.

"Do you want anything to eat?" she said.

"No thanks."

She walked to the stove and turned the gas up. Her rubber band had slid down her ponytail. She came to the refrigerator and nudged me. She took a coffee can out and a tin of shortbread, and I saw that they kept everything in there, even their bread and ketchup. It was big enough though.

She spooned the coffee in a pitcher and dumped the water in. We went to the table and sat across from each other. She pushed a rod down through the coffee and poured it. The wind blew hard outside. Some viny branches rapped the big bay window.

"You don't have to stay up with me," she said. "I'm wound up after work."

She tried some coffee. It was hot, and she pulled back from it and licked her lips.

"Have some shortbread," she said.

"I'm full."

I looked at everything but her.

"Did you see a lot of snakes in the woods?" she asked.

"I don't know."

"Sure you know. Did you see a lot?"

She would want to know everything about the fugitive life. But at first I didn't know what she was talking about. I shrugged.

"What would you have done if you would have gotten bit?"

"I don't know."

"Did you ever think about it?"

"No."

"Did you see any coyotes?"

"Sure."

"Bobcats?"

"Heard them."

"Do they really sound like babies crying at night?"

"More like a woman," I said.

I tried some coffee. She kept looking at me.

"Why did you come to Birmingham?" she said.

"I'm not sure."

"Why did you stay in Alabama?"

"Why have you?"

She laughed. "Aren't you hot in that big coat?"

I tried the zipper again, but it stayed stuck. So I pulled the back of the collar over my head and put it on the floor. She held her mug up and asked me if I liked it. I did. It was better than coffee.

"I like it with brown sugar," she said.

"Mine's gone."

She got up and microwaved some more milk. While she waited for it, she pulled the newspaper out from under the stack of mail.

"Was it really cold at night?" she said.

"No."

"Where did you sleep?"

"I don't know. We stayed with some people. Or we'd sleep in the leaves or in a field. We'd make a fire and lay around it."

She sat down. But she couldn't be still. She kept sliding her hands across the table, like a child smoothing dirt.

"I know this will sound strange," she said. "But when I read about y'all the whole thing sounded kind of appealing. I know that makes everything you've gone through sound cheap, and I don't mean to do that, but just being out there, walking, sounds kind of nice."

I could look at her when she was looking down. She went on:

"When I was a little girl, I wanted to be Huck Finn. I wanted to take off with our maid, Miss Yvette, and float on the rivers all the way to New Orleans. I would draw pictures of rafts with little tents on them. I asked for overalls for my tenth birthday and refused to wear a shirt underneath. It embarrassed my mom when her friends came over."

She stirred some sugar in my mug. She put the spoon on the table and the coffee puddled around it. It made me yawn. She said I should go to bed.

"What about all those trucks out in front of your bar?" I said.

She didn't understand. "What about them?"

"I don't know. All those golfer boys. Do they drive those farm trucks? And why do they put those stickers on the back about the Old South and cotton farmers?"

"Why do you ask that?"

"I don't know."

"I think I know what you mean," she said. "It doesn't make sense. But don't think I'm like them. Okay?"

I shrugged.

"Why did you ask that?"

"I don't know."

She rubbed her hand up her arm and rolled her shoulders. She seemed a long way off. I went to the counter and spread the paper. The story was on the first page, at the bottom. Some woman from Birmingham had gone down to write about us. She wrote:

> *Somewhere in Alabama, Robyn Banks' husband is wandering. She sits on the sofa with her cat, drinking a 7-Up. When she finishes, she will pick up her cordless phone and call the county sheriff for the second time today.*
>
> *"Why haven't they found him?" she says. "He is a helpless man. He can't take care of himself."*
>
> *In the two and a half months since he disappeared, she has woken nightly to the dreamt sound of a single gunshot. It sounds like the one that left her friend, John C. Raymond, slumped in her lap in the backseat of her car. That night, Sept. 12, she crawled out from under his body in time to see her husband's truck race up Highway 431, she says.*
>
> *Local and state law authorities have been unable to find the man, Gideon Banks, despite evidence that suggests he has been traveling through the state on foot with his adopted son and an elderly black man known for cultivating his churchyard with turnips.*
>
> *Miraculously, Raymond lived. The bullet, a .22, slid off the side of his head, just above his ear. His skull was fractured. But a week later he answered the roll call at the Phenix City City Council.*

There was stuff about the flawed investigation. That they never thought we'd be traveling with John Frederick, that Gid had always sworn his hate for him, and Robyn never thought we'd all three be knocking around. Then someone in Buena Vista had sworn they saw me and Gid in a blue Taurus with a blond woman at a gas station. They said we looked tired or drunk, and we bought a road map of Florida and a case of beer. Then:

> *Merit Banks was born in Tobbleton, Georgia, to Donnie and Julie Dunn, high school dropouts who worked odd jobs, often together. They telephoned catfish (an illegal means of shocking fish to the water's surface so they can be netted instead of hooked), were arrested several times for drag racing, and when Julie bore them a son, they named him for their favorite brand of cigarettes: Merit.*
>
> *In April of 1993, when Merit was eight, police showed up at the family's remote trailer-home with a search warrant for marijuana. After no one answered their knocks, they entered by force through the locked door. They found Donnie and Julie dead on the kitchen floor, both killed by a single shotgun blast. The gun was lying on the linoleum.*
>
> *Merit was found in his room, playing with toys. He had urinated in the corner of his room, police said. He had taken his sheets and comforter and slept under his bed.*
>
> *The couple had been dead two days, the coroner determined. Merit was placed in a foster home, where he refused to talk. More than that, he showed no outward emotion. Meanwhile, a reporter at the local paper discovered from forensic reports that the child's fingerprints were on the gun, along with both of his parents'. It became a topic of conversation in the county. Could the child be the killer?*
>
> *Police ruled the deaths an accident, but town residents continued to talk. The story gained footing up and down the Chattahoochee River, which separates Georgia from Alabama*

in the southern half of the states. When Gideon heard, he abruptly drove to Tobbleton and requested to adopt the boy. Robyn had reluctantly agreed. The couple had tried to have a child of their own for several years.

It talked about Gid and the governor and said that there were probably plenty of people willing to shelter us because of his avid opposition to the tax referendum.

After a while it got to John Frederick.

Little is known about the relationship between Merit and John Frederick White.

"They'd pull up in the old man's car and just sit out front and watch the girls go by," said Horace Green, who owns a convenience store where the man and the boy often came. "The kid would come in and buy a Dr. Pepper and some things. He never said nothing. Of course, I knew who he was, so I didn't say nothin' either. Then they'd just sit in the car half the day. Didn't look like they were talking. I'd see the old man asleep in there most of the time."

When Merit was adopted, he wasn't receptive to affection, Robyn said. He spent long amounts of time in the woods. He would bring home smooth rocks and put them on the shelves in his room.

After several years they discovered that Merit had begun to hang around with a man who he had apparently found one day while walking through the woods. The man lived simply, plowing fields here and there for a little money, growing vegetables in the churchyard for a "reward in heaven."

"John Frederick was a sweet man, a gentleman. I never heard him say one word unkind and I never heard anyone say a word unkind about him," said Verner Nail, a member of the Fishers of Men A.M.E., who was also acquainted with Merit. "I

don't know why he went around with that boy. And I don't know why that boy went around with him. No one ever knowed."

Robyn said she and her husband were leery of the relationship, but decided it was better for Merit to have one person who he was comfortable around. The boy could get anxious in crowds, she said. He would shake, and several times, he fainted.

"He made friends at first," she said. "But he got worse. In a couple of years, for all practical purposes, he was a complete mute. He'd go weeks without saying anything and he got in fights at school. We had to bring him out before the seventh grade. They wanted to send him to military school. I was for it, but Gid said, 'No.'"

I looked at the window when I finished. In the reflection I could see her looking at me.

"They could have found a better picture of you," she said after a while.

It was one someone had made me get in at a family reunion a couple of years back. The paper had cut out the others and zoomed in on my head.

We walked outside, went around the pool, and into a little stone pool house with rafters and a loft. She turned the lights on and an old bulldog came out from behind the counter.

"We woke him up," she said.

She called him Buck. He put his head against her leg and made noises. I got down on a knee and he came and put his head against my thigh. I grabbed the wrinkles on his neck.

"You should sleep in my bed," she said. "I'll stay down here on the couch."

"That's all right."

"Stay up there, Merit. You need it more than me."

She showed me to the bathroom and gave me a new toothbrush. On the handle it said, "Dr. Donald T. Snow, D.D.S." I brushed my teeth and washed my face. When I came out, she had changed clothes. Her hair was down. She said good night and went to the sink.

"Hey," I said.

"It's Haley."

"Yeah."

She waited.

"Gid doesn't know that he didn't do it," I said.

"Didn't do what?"

"He thinks he killed that boy."

Her head wrinkled a little. She leaned against the wall and folded her arms. "Did you know?" she said.

"I've known for a while."

I went up the ladder to her loft. The sheets were pulled down and there was a little light on the headboard. I got down to my long johns, put my clothes in the corner, and got in. The sheets were cool on my back and smelt like lotion. I turned the light off and listened to the water going through the pipes.

4.

IN THE MORNING I LAY THERE AND LISTENED TO HER BREATHING. THE wall was cool against my leg, and I went in and out of sleep for a while. Then I sat up and looked at her. The blankets were piled and twisted around her and she seemed very small. One pant leg had ridden up and the skin on her knee was rough and lined. It looked like a piece of shriveled fruit, and I thought that maybe she wasn't lying about all the time she had spent climbing trees and digging dirt.

I got my clothes and climbed down the ladder. I went through the garden to the other house. I was halfway across the kitchen before I saw the footprints on the tile. They drug in from the hallway, made a small circle, and went back out. I rubbed my fingers in one and smelt it. I decided to track him. There was a big streak down the hallway rug. He had taken a few steps into each room, maybe looking for me. The prints led into a big bedroom. I peeked in the bathroom and saw him standing in a bathtub. He was hunched over the faucet, cupping the water and tossing it on his chest and over his bent shoulders. His clothes were on the floor. He looked at the door and I ducked away.

There was a leather chair in the corner, and a photo album beside it. I looked at all the pictures. They were mostly from the beach, when she was young.

John Frederick came out with his shirt buttoned to the top. He rubbed his neck under his chin.

"Yes sir," he said. "I got the joy of the morning. You got it too?"

I went to him and gave him my hand. He held it in both of his.

"Do you know that in the mirror I saw my beard. And I said to myself, 'John Frederick, if it gets any more whiter, then you are gonna look like Moses.' But not yet. My beard is not white all through and I won't need a cane like he did. Not yet."

Gid had poked his head in the room. "Morning," he said, and went back out.

We went in the kitchen. I took some bread from the fridge and made some toast. They stood next to each other and looked around. I told them to sit at the table. I put some water on the stove and buttered the bread.

"I took a shower last night," Gid said. "Almost decided to sleep in there. It's got a big damn marble bench and a button that makes steam come out the walls. And that was just the kids' bathroom. Oh, and there was a button that made the floors heat. It's like some sort of resort."

I cleaned the grains out of the coffee pitcher and figured out how she had got it to work.

"How long you believe we can stay here?" Gid asked.

"We need to go," I said.

"What day is it?"

"Tuesday, maybe, or Wednesday."

"Where's the girl?"

I pointed through the window to the pool house.

"I think she's all right," he said.

I pushed the rod down through the coffee.

"Junior?"

"Yeah."

"I got something else to ask you."

I turned around.

"You think she'd mind if I got in that big whirlypool out back?

I'd promise not to piss in it."

John Frederick went to coughing hard, sticking his tongue out, and finishing each fit on some musical note.

"You okay, old boy?" Gid said.

"I got a bug in my throat."

I looked at some copper pots hanging on a rack. The bottoms hadn't been burned. Then Gid was beside me, reaching for the paper. He unfolded it and ran his palm slowly up the page, flattening the crease. He read a little and looked up.

"You seen this?"

I nodded.

"Some shit."

I poured some more coffee and sat on the sofa. Gid followed his finger across the lines. Then he came to it and it was just like I thought.

"Son of a bitch," he said, and he looked at me. "You seen it?"

His finger shook, and after a few lines he had to go back and trace them again. He folded the paper and went upstairs.

John Frederick drank the milk I had warmed him and his throat took it easy for a while. But the chair wasn't suited for him. The cushion kept sliding on him and then he'd be on the lip of the seat. I couldn't stop staring at him, remembering him in another place, sitting by his field with the early evening sun on his eyes, a pile of pecans in his lap, and a plastic bag blowing on the arm of his lawn chair.

When he fell asleep, I found a vacuum and erased his tracks. Then I walked through the house. It seemed like every room should have a velvet rope in front of it and a little sign with the history of the furniture. There were a lot more pictures and portraits of her than her brother. Maybe three times as many.

I found Gid on Morgan's floor. But he was doing more than lying. His hands were flat out and his fingers were white with pressure. And he was doing the same thing with his forehead, pushing.

I stepped over him and went in the bathroom. There was an uphol-
stered chair in the corner with a reading lamp beside it. Above it was
a picture of a Labrador with a mallard in its mouth. I turned both
showerheads on and waited for the water to run warm. In the mirror I looked at my ribs. I flexed my arms.

  In the shower I turned the heads on the marble bench. One I
put a little cooler, the other a little hotter. I lay face down under it
and wondered if Gid was just gonna shut down. Every man in his
family had either died for what was right, or killed for it, and Gid
had hoped that getting that councilman was equal to it. But that
man was still alive, and now Gid had felled himself, and I lay there
worrying I'd have to carry him out of there.

  I smelt my clothes before I reached for them. I hadn't noticed
until then. They smelt like a city. In the closet I found a T-shirt and
some pajama pants that still had the tags on them. I cinched the
drawstrings, then stepped over Gid and went to find the girl.

  In the pool house I heard the whip of the shower curtain. And
the mirror open and close. I sat on the hearth in front of a fire with
fake logs. She came out, wringing her hair with her hands.

  "Nice pants," she said.

  "They're your brother's."

  She had this skirt on with pockets on the front. She sat on the
couch and put her hands in them.

  "I always sleep too late," she said. "How long have you been up?"

  "Not too long."

  "Are the boys awake?"

  "They were."

  She crossed her legs. "Did you sleep all right?"

  "I can't remember."

  "I couldn't sleep on this couch. I hope I didn't wake you."

  She slid a rubber band off her wrist and put her hair back.

  "What time are you leaving?" she asked.

  "Whenever it starts raining."

"Why's that?"

"So the hounds can't sniff us."

"Well, there's a bakery nearby that has these muffins. Can I take you there before you leave?"

We got in the car. The houses we passed looked bigger in the daylight. I imagined everyone inside them laying in big sauna showers, or talking to their portraits. Some Mexicans in matching T-shirts raked some leaves. The girl yawned and put her foot up on the dash.

We came into town and pulled into a parking lot. There was a strip mall with a wood shingle roof. We parked in the middle of the lot, away from the other cars. She left the motor running and told me to wait. As she walked away, the wind blew her skirt like a curtain.

Coming back some guy spotted her. She gave him a hug and they talked.

We took a different way back. She took a long time at each stop sign. Then she stopped on the side of some neighborhood street and said we should share a muffin while they were still hot. I got the thing all over my hands trying to break it. Butter dripped from the middle.

She was a talker. She started into this thing about tree houses and wanted to know my opinion on them. It was like she thought I was some kind of woodsman, someone who could talk to animals, and live like them.

"I have a plan to get away from here," she said.

I folded the muffin wrapper and put it in the bag.

"It was good," I said.

"Good. Will you tell me what you think of my plan? Honestly. I told a couple of people more than a year ago and they laughed at me. You won't do that?"

"I won't."

"All right. So my grandmother died a couple of years ago and left me some money. It's not a fortune but it's enough to live really simply on for a long time. And I've been researching what it would take to move a long way from here and live out in the woods."

"Have you ever been in the woods?"

"Wait," she said. "You can buy cheap land on these inlets in Vancouver. There's no one around and you have to get to the shore by a little boat. The forest is made up of giant sycamores, or something like that, and the woods come right up to the water. I read about these friends who built this round, two-story house around one of the trees. Way up high. None of them were builders either. Now they go back there every year for a week or two. I want to do what they did but I don't want to make it a vacation house. I want to stay there."

I thought of Rodney Jones and wondered if he had been as normal as her. But I looked at her and tried say that it was a good idea.

"That'd be all right," I said.

"I'm gonna do it soon," she said.

A lawn sprinkler hit my window and gave me a start.

"You see what I mean?" she said. "They're watering in November. And it rained a foot last night. I don't know if I can live in a place like this."

She turned the radio up and we were driving. In a yard I saw some more Mexicans in matching T-shirts. They were raking leaves, but I imagined they were dollar bills. I thought of the girl doing labor. Trying to hammer, trying to saw, trying to hermit herself from extravagance. But I didn't think her plan would help her much. You can't be poor if there's no one else around.

"So you think I could pull it off?" she said.

"Maybe you could. I don't know. What about college?"

"I did that already. I finished in two years. My parents want me to go to UAB for med school. They just want me to stay at home."

We found John Frederick as I had left him. His hands were folded and his head was bowed. Haley went to him.

"How you feeling this morning? How's that cough?" she said.

"Oh. All right. Yeah. It's a good morning." His voice was rough and flat, like the voice from the storm speakers that tells you where the tornadoes are headed. He lifted his arm across his chest and set his hand on top of hers. But he pulled it away to cover his mouth.

"I don't like the way that sounds," she said. "Here. We got you a muffin. I'm going to look for some cough medicine."

I microwaved him some milk. She came back with the syrup and I went to look for Gid. I found him on the floor with his eyes open. I set the muffin on the bedside table and took a seat in a chair by the window.

"Do you want a pillow?" I asked.

He didn't say anything. He just stared up at the ceiling and blinked.

"That's nice," I said. "You want to hear a story?"

He put his arm over his eyes.

"You do?" I said. "Good. Let me think of one."

I picked a crumb of sugar from the muffin.

"All right," I said. "I got one. Do you remember when that possum got in the trash can and Robyn made me kill it? Nod for me if you do. Well, I know you do. You remember I shot it with a .22 and put a hole in the can? She told me to wrap it in a bag and leave it in there. I didn't want to kill the thing, but she made me. So that night I got it out and wedged it in the motor block of her car. You remember how she thought a squirrel had died in there? It made her clothes smell."

He rolled over, and I remembered the night in September when I found him on the kitchen floor. Finally he said, "I don't like them things she said about you."

"Who?"

"My wife."

"You want your muffin now?"

"It's her I should have got."

"I'll heat it up for you."

"I ain't hungry." He lifted his head and there was a carpet print on his face. "Does that woman smoke?"

5.

HALEY HAD THE OLD MAN LAUGHING. I STOOD IN THE HALL AND LISTENED.

"Look, John Frederick. I really hugged them," she said. "And I screamed at my dad, and they flopped out of my arms."

She was telling him all about her summers at the lake and showing him pictures. Everything about them sounded nice, but she couldn't tell one without dropping something bad in.

"Look. Here's my brother when he was twelve. He was no good at baseball but he played because my Dad wanted him to. He's always felt like he couldn't do anything good enough for them. He's always apologizing to them for being a bad kid. I worry about him, John Frederick. He lives in Tuscaloosa and he's in a little bit of trouble. I feel like I need to stay near home in case anything happens to him."

"That's right."

"You think so?"

"Oh yeah."

"But haven't you ever wanted to get away from home?"

"You know I habn't been home yet."

"Not since September?"

"Not since eber. When I was a boy, I would watch the train ride by and I'd want to hang on the side and go find a new place. I was a stranger in my own house. In my own town too. I still am. But I learned not to hunt around for a home here because it's neber gonna feel like I want it to."

"I think I know what you mean," she said. "But I don't know if I like it."

I was still sitting in the hall. She told him she would fix him some soup. I went in the kitchen then and took her seat. I shut the album and watched her move about the kitchen. She had to guess where certain things were. She was having trouble with the can opener so I got up and took it. I popped open several cans of clam chowder and poured them in the pot.

She fixed us bowls and set out a plate of saltines.

"You're impressed?" she said. I said I was. She tried it too and said, "It doesn't have any taste, does it?"

"Maybe if you had some salt," I said.

"That's what the crackers are for."

John Frederick ate like usual. He could chew a cracker for a full minute.

"Mom never cooked," she said. "I was raised on Davenport's pizza. Dad would hardly eat anything else."

John Frederick got up and left.

"Where's he going?" she said.

I shrugged.

"Do you think he's all right? With that cough?"

"I don't know."

"I felt his shoulders and they didn't seem too hot." She slid the photo album towards her and put it on a chair. "I don't like to look at pictures of me when I was little. My eyes have looked this way since I was a kid. I've had this same look."

We were quiet for a minute. Then she said, "What about you? Do you like to look at your baby pictures?"

I finished my soup. She said she was sorry. I shrugged, and I went to get another bowl. While I was over the pot, the phone rang. I dropped the bowl in and had to fish it out.

"Daddy," she said.

I rinsed the bowl and listened. Everything seemed nice between them. He was talking most of the time and she kept laughing. But when she hung up, she looked like she was ready for bed. She joined me at the table and asked me about my second serving. I said it was better than the first, that the flavor had gotten richer with time. But she didn't seem to listen. She just said that her dad at least worked a job. He was a dentist. And a lot of people she knew had dads that hadn't ever worked. And her mom volunteered at the Alabama Shakespeare Theatre. That was better than nothing.

"How high do you want it to be?" I said.

It was like I had woken her. She sat up straighter and rubbed her eyes.

"Sorry. What'd you say?"

"How high will you live in the tree?" I said.

"Oh. Real high. I want to spit and not hear it land."

"Will you be able to sit still up there?"

"That's the only thing I'm good at. Are you making fun of my plan?"

"I'm not. But how will you stay warm in the winter?"

"A stove."

"What about when you want to leave? How will you get out of the woods?

"I'll e-mail a boat driver to come pick me up."

"E-mail?"

"I'll run power on a generator when I need it. I can get a satellite Internet hookup."

"E-mail in a tree fort?"

"Tree house."

"That's like Huck Finn having a motor."

"If motors were around, he would have had one."

"Like hell he would've."

I said it too seriously, and she grinned.

"Yeah," she said. "He would have stolen one."

I thought about that. "No," I said. "He wasn't in a hurry."

"I think he was."

She told me she had a book that could tell her how to build it. So we went out across the garden to the pool house. The book was on the coffee table, below some others. She opened it and set it across our laps. There were pictures of a bunch of guys hanging in harnesses up in a tree. And there were floor plans and photos of the finished thing. She told me how she could make it better; a bathtub by this window, a skylight here. But I wasn't really able to concentrate. If she mentioned some picture or dimension, I would point to it like some toddler identifying animals in a children's book. She would pull my hand away when she wanted to turn the page and then set it back. She talked all the time but I was only totally conscious of two things: a slight whistle I discovered in her voice. And the weight of the book across the lap of my pajama pants.

"You're falling asleep on me," she said. I wasn't. "Take a nap. I might take one too."

She went to the bathroom. I set the book on the table and pulled my feet up. They were warm on the place where she had sat. She came back and fell into the other corner. Her legs swung up over mine and she buried her feet in a cushion.

"I don't know why the story practically called you a mute," she said.

I shrugged. "I don't know why I'm this way."

"What way?"

"Quiet."

"But you're not at all. That's what I'm asking. Why did that lady write that?"

"Gid and Robyn thought I was at first. So did my teachers. When they asked me to try and say things, I couldn't."

"You wouldn't."

"No."

"Did you ever say stuff when you were by yourself?"

"In the woods. Yeah."

"What would you say?

"I'd sing John Frederick's songs. But not the words at first. I'd only hum, and maybe I'd let a word or two in. Then after a while I would talk to Gid more. But never to Robyn much."

"Did you meet John Frederick right after you got there?"

"Yeah. But I spied on him for a long time. Then one day his hat blew off and it was like he didn't even know. It was the damnedest thing. And it was tumbling over the field towards this little muck pond and I just broke out of the woods and ran and got it and took it to him."

"Were you in the woods a lot?"

"Yeah."

"And you never built a tree house?"

"No."

"Never even tried?"

Her hair was in her eyes.

"The story got it all wrong," she said. "It's not a voice you lack. It's an imagination."

I grabbed her ankle then. It was smooth.

6.

I REMEMBER EVERY MINUTE OF THOSE DAYS. I TURN THEM OVER LIKE A dead field. But I know that they are gone, that what has withered should be plowed under. But damn if I can stop remembering, stop muttering, stop wishing I would have ever known anything different than walking around the woods, and sitting below a shade tree with an old man, and that the height of romance was to be alone on a flipped bucket, watching catfish and carp poke their faces into the moonlight.

Auburn and Alabama are playing on the TV. Why have I turned the game on? I don't care about it. But sometimes I stop remembering and watch the offensive linemen break the huddle and jog to the line of scrimmage. It's the best part.

I have made some coffee. Later I may have a beer or two. And I will try to watch the game and think about nothing.

Cadillac Williams. Cadillac Williams. There has never been a name so good. Not for a ball carrier, at least, and every time I hear the TV man say it, it does something to me. If the boy stays healthy, he will be able to buy a Cadillac for every day of the week. Merit Banks. Merit Banks. I never knew I was named for a cigarette. Cadillac Banks. Merit Williams.

7.

THE AFTERNOON GOT AWAY QUICK. SHE SLEPT A LITTLE, AND AFTER A WHILE I realized that little hairs had poked through on her leg. They felt like sand.

She asked me a lot about Gid, and I told her what I knew. She wanted to understand why he could be upset that the man hadn't died. I tried to tell her that he wasn't. That he was worked up because he *couldn't* kill.

"Should we check on him?" she said.

"No. Let's let him be."

"C'mon," she said, and she pulled me up.

We walked upstairs. Gid was in the big chair in the corner of Morgan's room. The floor was wet where he had been lying. The rug was sopped and there was a puddle on the wood.

"Junior," he said. He had a book on his lap and his shirt was wet.

"You been reading?" I said.

"I haven't been," he said. "Just picked the one that felt the best in my hands. I like the smell of the thing too. The old ones remind me of something."

The girl sat on the bed.

"How are you, Gid?" she asked.

"Little lady, how are you?"

"I'm all right." She pulled some hair from her face. "I'm tired.

But I'll be okay."

"It's hard being you," he said. "We don't want to see you get worn down."

"Thank you."

"We'd hate to blame ourselves."

"Don't."

"Listen, little one. Do you need to go to work tonight? Because, and I'm being serious, we can go."

"I'm off tonight."

"And it's not gonna trouble you if we stay?"

"You can't leave yet."

"Well, we can't move in either. Not unless you ask."

"I know."

"I do have something to ask you," he said.

"Sure."

"Let me just say first that all these years I've done my best to be a man of responsibility and duty. But I've realized here lately that you were born to take care of a good man. You've got all the grace and patience to keep a man in order. To keep him from getting lost in himself. That's what a good woman does." He cleared his throat.

"I've decided today that I'll never be the woman that you are. So I want to ask you, when I go away, will you look after John Frederick?"

Haley looked at me. Gid had his head hung back and his tongue was wagging. I had forgotten that he could laugh that way.

"Junior," he said. "Fetch me that muffin. I almost forgot about it."

I hopped down and took it to him.

"Hey miss," he said. "I got something else to ask you. All these paintings of wildlife. Does your family like to hunt?"

"Dad and Morgan do," she said. "They tried to take me, but I would never go."

"And I seen some gun cases in here but no guns."

"Dad had to put them in storage. What about you Gid, you like to hunt?"

"Rich people deer hunt. And they shoot ducks. All of that they can do hiding out in a blind. But poor folks trap. And they coon hunt."

"Why's that?"

"Because their clothes ain't warm enough to sit still."

"Really?" she said. "So which do you do?"

"Neither."

"You don't like killing things?"

"No. That's not it. It's just that my clothes are too warm to go running around the woods, but I can't sit still for long. I got too much energy."

She smirked at him.

"I'm serious, miss."

"I made some supper, Gid," she said. "New England clam chowder. Ask Junior here to tell you how fine it was."

"Yeah, Junior? Tell us what you know of New England."

I leaned over against the headboard.

"He doesn't want to flatter me," she said. "But he loved it. He cried right in his bowl."

"Did John Frederick eat it?"

"Through a straw."

"I like you little lady. Let's get married."

"That's sad, Gid. I'm a lesbian."

"Yeah? And I'm a woman."

"Is that true?" she looked at me. I nodded.

"Really miss. Will you marry me?"

"Of course. If you can tell me my name."

She had him. He was red, and he pretended to read his book. Then he said, "You're a smart one. You'll make for a good wife. Junior, you can be best man. We'll all live in a house that smells like muffins."

We heard the coughing as we went downstairs. Haley looked at us over her shoulder. In the kitchen it was Gid who went to him. He put his hand on the old man's back.

"Hey old fellow, you gonna be all right?"

John Frederick stared at Gid's shirt. It was damp across the shoulder and across the back.

"We're all getting kind of worried about you," Gid said. "You don't sound so good. Did you take any of this medicine here?"

The old man stared.

"Do you want to lay down?" Haley asked. "You've been at this table a long time."

"It's been a long time?" he said. "Oh yeah. Yes it has."

"I could put a movie on in the TV room. There's better chairs for resting."

He pushed away from the table. She took his hand. We followed them through the house. She put the old man in a big recliner. Gid took a seat in the other one. She chose a movie about fishing. As she messed with the machine, John Frederick said, "Ma'am. I wonder if you hab a mirror I can hold in my hand?"

She looked at me.

"Sure," she said. "My mom has one. I'll go get it."

"I do thank you."

John Frederick got up and spun the recliner so that it faced away from the TV. Then it was Gid wanting me to explain. I knew, but I made like I didn't. The girl came back.

"I don't have to play a movie," she said.

He reached for the mirror. She gave it to him. He held it up at an angle so that he could see the screen over his shoulder. She knelt down beside him and whispered something. Gid leaned over to listen.

John Frederick said, "If you see straight into that machine, it will burn your eyes up. That's why you need to watch it in back."

She squeezed his arm. "I never knew that."

"Oh yeah," he said.

Gid pulled the lever on the side of the chair. Laying back, he could see the old man looking into the reflection. He was still watching him when the girl led me out of the room.

8.

WE STOOD IN THE KITCHEN.

"I want to take you somewhere," she said. "Just for a little while."

I took a step back. There was a clock ticking that I hadn't heard before.

"I'll go tell Gid," I said.

"I'll tell him. Just put your shoes on. And I washed your overalls. They're by the door."

I slid the pants on and Velcroed my shoes. There was a backpack there. She handed it to me and buttoned her coat. We got in her car and went down the same streets we had taken earlier. She didn't say anything. The pavement had dried and she took the turns fast. When we came into town, she swung into a parking spot and told me to wait. She went into a pizza place and came out just as fast. She set the box on my lap.

We backtracked all the way, and the girl was quiet. But she didn't slow as we neared her place. Instead she cut the motor a few minutes later on a dark street and told me to hop out. I held the pizza and she grabbed the backpack. I followed her into the grass. She stopped on a path and let me draw even with her.

"Dad plays golf out here," she said. "It's a messed-up place. But it's nice at night."

We walked and the wind blew through the gap in my coat. The grass was smooth. It rose and fell like rocking water. She led me off the path and down a hill to a gulch. Behind it was a wall of pine trees. In the middle was a green. She went to the center and pulled the flag pole. She tossed it to the side and shrugged the backpack from her shoulders.

"Here. Help me lay this down," she said, handing me one side of a big blanket. I felt the ground. "It drains fast," she said. "It's sand underneath."

Then she pulled out two sleeping bags stuffed in little sacks. She fitted the zipper of one to the zipper of the other, and made them into one big thing.

"Take your shoes off," she said as she undid her laces. I kicked them off and stood on the blanket. She pulled a bottle of wine out and went to work with a corkscrew. She flipped the cork and stuck it back in the bottle. We pulled the sleeping bags up around our legs and I set the pizza across us. The bottle was behind us, in the flag cup.

She separated the pizza down the middle and said, "That's your side."

It was cut into little squares, and when I tasted it, I knew why she had said it. She took a sip of wine and handed it to me. I had never tasted real wine before. Only some strawberry stuff someone had passed me at one of Gid's art festivals. She laughed at the face I made.

"Are you a golfer?" I said.

"I played tennis for a while. I used to be good. But never golf. Once Dad let me drive the cart. I might have been ten. And the course ranger came up and gave him a fine. He pays so much to be a member here, mainly just to eat brunch on Sundays, and they fine him for letting his daughter drive a go-cart."

She couldn't finish her side. She crawled down in the sack so that only her head stuck out. I ate slowly and stared out across the lawn.

"Are you cold, Merit?" she said.

"Not very cold."

The wine wasn't so sour anymore.

"Why don't you take that big coat off?"

"I stole this coat."

"It's a nice one."

"It smells like deer piss."

"Did you get it from a deer hunter?"

"Yeah."

"So he was rich."

"No. Gid was making all that up."

I pulled my coat off. The sleeping bag wasn't as big as it looked. I couldn't figure out where to put my hands. I fidgeted.

"There's a zipper down the middle," she said. "Stick to your side."

I grabbed her arm. She put her foot up on my leg.

"I forget I'm in Birmingham when I'm here," she said.

We lay quietly for a long time. The wine was working on me.

"I started coming out here when I was thirteen. I would ride my bike and pack a blanket. This is the best spot because you can't see any lights. Are you comfortable?"

"Yeah."

"What are you thinking about?"

"I'm not."

She crawled out a little ways and took a shot of wine.

"I went online today and saw some more stories about y'all."

"How was my picture?"

"The same. The stories were all pretty short. Said an old lady at the Salvation Army thinks she saw you yesterday, and a homeless man downtown. They also said that Gid has a lot of friends from his travels around the state and someone might be putting y'all up."

She was propped on her elbows. Her hair hung in front of her shoulders.

"Did Gid really make a lot of friends this summer?" she said.

"No."

"Did you vote for the tax plan?"

"No."

"Why not?"

"I'm not registered and I don't care."

"I voted for it. My parents said if I had earned a lot of money I would think different."

"Would you?"

"I hope not. But I'm scared I would."

"So you'll live in a tree house?" I said.

"Yes."

"And when you get tired of reading by the stove, you'll go read in the bathtub?

"Yes."

"And you'll be able to go without your fancy pizza?"

"That's the thing keeping me here."

She pushed me on the shoulder. I was looking at the sky.

"You loved that pizza," she said. "You tried to steal from my half."

"Hand me that wine."

She took a shot and gave it to me. I leaned up on my elbow and tipped it back.

"Are you afraid of getting arrested?" she said.

"No." I thought for a minute. "Are you?"

She laughed. "No. They can't catch me."

"I'm more afraid of freezing to death. I'm scared we're killing John Frederick."

"I love that man," she said. "He'll be fine."

"Gid's acting different."

"Better?"

"When we went up there to check on him, he was a different person. All easygoing. But I don't know if that's better or not."

"Why not?"

"I can't believe how he was acting, really. He ain't the kind that can talk himself down, not even about the smallest thing. And there he was with all that built-up stuff piled on him. Like all he ever thought was true wasn't anymore. He didn't move for five, six hours. Then we go up there and he's happy as spring."

"What do you think he'll do?"

"And it was the first time he ever called John Frederick by his name. He's never done that before. Anyway, I can't figure what happened. Normally, when he's like that, all stormed over, the only thing that can get him out of it is anger. By being madder at something than he is at himself. But he wasn't upset at all. I don't know what he'll do, what we'll all do. But I don't think we're gonna go out wandering again."

"If you do, will you take me?"

"No."

"I didn't think so."

"You wouldn't go."

She took another shot and wiped her lips with the back of her hand. She told me about her family for a while. She said her brother was cracking up and her parents didn't know how to deal with him. I thought it sounded like her parents were the crack-ups. But I didn't think any of it was really bad. She just cared too much.

She was a little worked up. She rolled into me. All I could think of was whether or not the hooks on my overalls were hurting her face. I pulled away some and looked at her. She laughed and rubbed her eyes.

"I'm sorry," she said.

I reached across her for the wine.

"Share," she said, and I handed her the bottle. She sat up and finished it.

The moon was high but little. More light came from the city than from the sky. It was yellow above the tree line. It looked like a week-old black eye.

"Sit up," she whispered.

Out across the lawn a few deer were walking towards the trees.

Something snapped in the woods. They stopped and sniffed the air. And their cupped ears waved like an actress or a queen. Then one of them bounded and the others followed. Their tails were tall and white, and as they disappeared into the trees, part of me wished I could do the same. Maybe it was the same for her. It was a long time before she lay back down. She shivered.

"We should go back now and make sure they're all right," she said.

"Yeah."

And a few hours later we did.

9.

THE COFFEE PITCHER WAS ON THE COUNTER WHEN WE GOT HOME. GID
had put it in the microwave and the metal had shorted it out. The
microwave door was open but the light was off. A note was under
the pitcher. It said:

John Frederick did it. Sorry, Gideon L. Banks.

Haley went to let her dog out and I went up to the TV room. I
found them both asleep in their chairs. John Frederick was still fac-
ing the wrong way. The mirror was on his lap and his hand was
wrapped around his throat. I went around to Gid. The TV screen lit
him up in blue. I pushed on the back of his chair as I pulled the lever
on the side.

"Damn, Junior," he said, sitting upright. "Damn you. I was having a dream about my college girl. You ruined it."

"You didn't go to college."

"But she did," he said.

"C'mon. Come up and go to bed."

"I blew out that woman's microwave. You think she'll kick us
out?"

"She only laughed."

"Rich people."

"Who's there?" John Frederick shouted. We jumped a little.

"It's me. Merit and Gid," I said.

"And the Holy Spirit," Gid said.

"Okay. Yes sir," he said, and went back to sleep.

I followed Gid to the kitchen.

He whispered, "Old boy almost coughed his soul up while you were gone. Once he jerked and hit the chair handle. It threw him up. When he fell asleep, I got to wondering if he had a fever. You know how my hands are. I can't feel nothing through them. So I bent down and stuck my cheek on his forehead. He's hotter than hell."

He looked at the floor for a minute, then said, "He needs to see a doctor. Every time he goes to coughing I feel like I'm the one who got him sick."

He looked me in the eye then to make sure I knew what he meant. And I shook my head to let him know that he wasn't thinking clearly. I put some water on the stove and stood there waiting for it to whistle.

I spooned some grounds in the coffee pitcher. The pot whistled and I poured it in.

"Damnedest contraption I've ever seen," Gid said.

The girl came in.

"I'm sorry, miss, about your microwave. I didn't mean to."

"It's fine, Gid. I'll have someone come fix it tomorrow."

"I'll pay you when I can."

"I charge interest."

"Listen. Why don't we get married? You can come see me in the prison and about the time you get tired of me then visitation will be over."

"Don't talk like that."

I spooned some sugar in the coffees and stirred it for a while.

"You can't talk like that," she said. "We're gonna get married and live in a little house by the sea."

"Okay, little one. And Junior can be our pool boy."

She draped her arm around my neck and looked down in the coffee.

She said, "You got to be sure the sugar's melted. Just keep at your stirring."

I stopped then. She took the spoon and put it in the sink.

"Is that second cup for me or for Gid?"

"I'll make you one."

She took his mug to the table.

"Are you old enough to work in that juke joint?" he asked her.

"I am now, but I wasn't when I started."

"Oh." I heard the clock.

"I'm just working there until I figure out what I'm gonna do with myself," she said. "I like a lot of stuff but I'm not good at anything. When did you find out you could make pottery?"

"Not till I was forty-something."

"Were you good at it from the start?"

"Pretty good. But I was just copying other stuff I saw. It took me a few years before I started making up my own creations."

"What were they?"

"Fine art mainly. Like a Harley man with a vulture on his shoulder, pecking at his eyes. Or a little shoeshine boy about to hammer a railroad spike through a sleeping man's wingtip shoes."

"You miss doing it?"

"No, I haven't. I never had too much fun at it. My wife never said she liked one thing I made. I wasn't allowed to keep it in the house. And I got to where I couldn't make anything without thinking the whole time what she would say about it."

"What would she say?"

"She never said nothing. She wouldn't even look at any of it. Acted like it embarrassed her. Every once in a while I'd do something that made me feel all right, but just for a second, 'cause I'd think of her and all the pleasure would bleed out of it."

"Do you miss her?" she asked.

"Once," he said, "I made a statue that looked just like her. And I put her in a white wedding dress and made her the shape she was when I met her. And right below her I made a sign that said, "I do solemnly vow to never make you feel like a fool ass." I sat it up in the shed for a while. But I got tired of looking at it so I pitched it in the pond."

I took the girl her coffee.

"Junior," Gid said. "Sit with us."

But I didn't like how easy he was acting. It bothered me. So I went up to the TV room and sat beside John Frederick. I spun the other chair around so that we both faced the door. He was staring flatly at the ceiling.

"What do you think?" I asked him.

He didn't seem to realize I was there.

"How was the movie?"

He just sat there. "I wish we were sitting in your car at the Green Store," I said. "Not in these big leather things. Once, while you were sleeping there, a bird flew in the car and sat on your steering wheel. And he watched you for ten minutes, maybe. Your hat was on your lap and a little bug was on it. When the bird saw it, he jumped down and ate it. Then he flew out. You started laughing in your sleep. And do you remember that time when I was still small and I got caught in the rain on the way to your place? When I got there, I was wet and you gave me a big wool blanket and a cup of milk. Was that butter-milk? I had never been in your trailer before. I wish we were back there. I know you say you don't miss it. But I wish we had never met any of these people and it was just me and you sitting in plastic chairs. Not these big leather things. I can't get comfortable in them because there's too much to think about.

"I think we're gonna take you to the doctor tomorrow. I'm not sure how it will all work out, but I'll stay with you.

"Oh yeah. You remember when that man looked in the Icebox and passed out? It wasn't a cat in there. It was a kid. Sometimes I wish I never knew that. I think about it too much and it feels like I miss the boy. But I don't even know who he was.

"It's the same with this girl. I wish I didn't know about her. She's a good person though. She knows some things and she likes you a lot. There's this thing with her. She always feels like she wants to go away. But she never does it."

He reached his hand across and put it on my wrist.

He said, "Did you know that all the time I lib in my trailer and you come to see me that I could look under my mat and find paper money almost any day? And I would gib thanks and put it in my pocket. Some dollars went in the plate and some I gib to you to buy what we need at the store. All that time it was that way."

His hand felt like hot mud on my wrist. He swallowed, then said: "If you know where to find a blanket, I would thank you. I might lay here tonight. I won't sleep much. No sir. I just wait up."

I found a few blankets in a little closet and brought them to him.

"Do you want us to take you to the doctor tomorrow?" I asked.

"If you want to do that, then that's okay."

"Do you want anything to eat? Something to drink?"

"Maybe a little milk."

I went down to the kitchen. Gid and the girl weren't there. I heated some milk on the stove and took it to the old man.

"All right," he said. "I do thank you."

I heard the shower running upstairs. I went up and stuck my head in the bathroom.

"Junior," Gid shouted. "I think I might go ahead and sleep in here."

"I think you should."

He opened the door a little and looked at me in the fogging mirror.

"How you holding up?"

"Okay."

What hair he had was matted on the sides of his face and he blinked a lot from the dripping water.

"What about the old man?"

"He's hot but he thinks he's cold."

"He'll get better."

"Yeah."

"Junior," he said even louder. I looked up. "I'm naked. Get."

I found Haley in the pool house. She was on the floor with her dog and a glass of wine. I sat down. The dog rolled over so I could scratch his stomach. I kneaded his shoulders like dough.

"Gid told me what the deal is tomorrow," she said. "Has he explained it all to you?"

"No." I lay back.

"There's a glass of wine over there," she said.

"I only drink from the bottle."

"The bottle's there too," she said.

I reached for the dog again. Her hand was there too. "I'm the reason that you're not still out there," she said.

I looked at her. "What do you mean?"

"You'd still be out there and it wouldn't be ending."

"Don't say things like that."

"Why not?"

"Because you make it sound like some western with campfire songs and sunsets."

"I know I do. But I'm still sorry."

"It was ending before we met you," I said. "It was."

We were quiet for a while. The dog got tired of us and went to bed.

"What are you going to do?" she asked.

"When?"

"When there's no more wandering."

"I'll hang around John Frederick."

"Forever?"

"Sure."

"Don't you get restless?"

"I don't."

"I wish I was that way."

"It's easy."

"How?"

"Just believe that things will always be about the same as they are now. No matter where you go. And that you'll always be about the same as you've always been."

"That's the way?"

I nodded.

"I'll never do that," she said.

She lay down and folded her hands across her stomach. "If that's really your secret then I'm sorry I know it. If I believed that, I'd give up."

I watched the firelight blowing on the ceiling. Then I said, "John Frederick has another way. But I can't figure it out."

"Do you think he's enlightened?"

"He's something."

"Will y'all let me come visit?"

I laughed.

"I'll bring my own chair," she said.

"You can come. You can sit with us and watch the clouds sail past and swing at the flies around your ears, and when the rain comes, you can come inside and sit on the sofa and watch the water drip into pans on the floor and hope that the tornado sirens are crying wolf. And before the ground gets hard again, you can sit on the wheel hub of John Frederick's tractor while he turns the earth."

"I like the way you talk. What else?"

"Well, we'll drink homemade strawberry milk a lot of the time and swim in pools of water that are thirty feet deep and clear to the bottom, and when it gets dark, we'll all three lay out in the yard, because there's a mini meteor shower almost every night."

"Really?"

"No. And the water's muddy and full of snakes."

"What about the milk?"

"I'll fix you some."

"Can I drive the tractor?"

"No."

"Will there be a place for me to sleep?"

"In the backseat of your car."

"Thank you, Merit."

"I forgot to tell you that John Frederick won't let women in his house."

"So I'll have to sit out in the rain?"

"In your car."

"Why doesn't he let girls inside?"

"He's worried about being an adulterer. He thinks he's still married. He drives around with these big fat ladies sometimes. But they never come inside."

"Maybe he'd let a skinny girl in."

"Maybe."

"You and me could get married and then I wouldn't be a threat."

"You need to stop hanging around Gid."

"I need to stop hanging around here."

"You need to stop saying that."

She rolled over.

"I don't know anything about it," I said. "I shouldn't have said that."

"It's fine," she said. "I'm tired of talking about it too."

She sat up and took some wine. I took her glass and finished it.

10.

It looks as if Auburn will win the game. Alabama doesn't have enough talent. They cheated a few years ago and got caught. They lost some scholarships, and they don't have the athletes they used to. The Auburn linemen feel like men. You can tell by the way they walk in between plays. They don't want the game to end.

So Auburn will win unless a miracle happens. And half of the state will feel like they have won too. The other half will sulk like children.

It used to be that two teams could tie. It happened some. But none of the fans could stand it. So they made overtime so people could always know who was better and who was worse. And who should feel good and who should feel bad because most people don't understand how nice it is to feel nothing.

I liked a tie. I liked to watch the fans all walk away trying to figure out what to feel. And to see all of the players looking relieved. Looking at their faces, you could always tell that love of victory is only a prettier way of saying fear of loss.

But the best part about a tie was that it kept people from embarrassing themselves. There were neither tears nor fist pumping.

Anyway, Auburn will win and the final score will be put on T-shirts that people will wear to rags. There will be some graphic of a tiger humiliating an elephant. But the feeling will be gone in a few days. Everyone will be back to counting their money, and their children, and their mistakes. They will only think about this game when they need a little pride. But it won't help much. And the rivalry will sleep until the papers predict the winners a year from now, and the people waken again to the persistence of loss.

11.

The girl nudged me. She had turned the fire off.

"We should get in the bed," she whispered. She held her hand out. I took it and she pulled me up. I was against her then. My sight adjusted and I could see her round eyes. I looked at them, one at a time.

"Let's go up," she said.

We went up the ladder to the loft. She pulled the chain on her bedside lamp, set it on the floor, and put a T-shirt over the shade so that the light was low and soft. It made everything nicer.

She went back down to brush her teeth. I lay on top of the covers and listened to the water in the pipes. They cut off and she came back up.

She crawled across the bed and lay her head on my arm.

"Did you ever have any friends besides John Frederick?" she said.

"Not since I left school."

"When you were thirteen."

"Yeah."

"So you've never had a girlfriend?"

"Not since the fifth grade."

She laughed. "What happened?"

"To us?"

"Yeah."

"She got a prosthetic leg and learned how to walk normal."

She lifted her head. I stared up at the neon stars glued to the ceiling.

"And that turned you off?"

"Leddy was her name. For Christmas, after the operation, the United Way sent her to the White House to meet Hillary Clinton, and she came back cool. Then her family moved to town so she wasn't on the country bus anymore."

"So you broke up?"

"We were never official."

She laughed. "Well, were you mad she got her leg?"

"She would always tell me how different it would be when she got it. I was happy about it then. But when she got it, everyone was always touching it. The guys would all pat her thigh and it felt like they were all touching her. I wasn't happy about it then. I thought it ruined her. She didn't need it."

"What did you say when you saw it?"

"Nothing."

I adjusted my arm underneath her. She took my hand and swung my arm out from under her and put it at my side. She rolled onto her side and pressed her forehead against my shoulder.

"Do you want to ask me anything?" she said.

I wanted to know how many guys she had laid against. It was hard to think of anything else. That T-shirt over the lamp was a trick she already knew. It wouldn't have helped me to hear if she had been nice to two boys or twelve. But I wanted the knowledge like hell. I was like a dog dying to bite a firecracker. Finally I asked her, "When is your birthday?"

"May. When's yours?"

"July. What will you get me?"

"A new coat. What will you get me?"

"A hammer."

"Thanks Merit."

"It's the only thing you don't have."

"Will you teach me how to use it?"

"You can practice on my thumb."

She stuck her fingers in my ribs so that I squirmed and wrestled her wrists. There was pressure and resistance, and then we were still.

"Merit?"

I looked at her.

"Do you think less of me because I have a lot of stuff?"

"I've hated rich people my whole life but now I'm not sure why."

"Your whole life?"

"Yeah. The rich kids didn't take the bus. Their moms would come to get them. I remember every day a minivan would come for this brother and sister. And there was a Labrador retriever that sat in the front. The kids sat in the back. I decided to hate it because I couldn't have it. I guess I've done that for everything."

"I don't like being rich," she said.

"What's so bad about it?"

"It does something to you. It limits you. I think you grow up thinking you deserve it all. And that puts you out of touch with everyone who's ever had to earn anything. Which is the entire rest of the world. So you only hang out with other rich people, and that's just dull. I think you're only as interesting as the people you know."

"How did you figure out you didn't deserve it?"

She thought for a minute.

"I knew Huck Finn was more deserving."

"So you started wearing jeans?"

"I'd take them off behind a shrub and rub holes in them with a rock."

"Do you wish you were born poor?"

"I don't know," she said. "But I wish I never had to see grown men pout all afternoon about a few missed putts. And I wish I never had to listen to a bunch of moms bragging about their daughters' boyfriends. And I wish I wouldn't get nervous every time I see a black man in a parked car at the grocery."

The way she looked at me, I didn't care anymore who had lay there before me. Our shadows were long on the wall, and sharp. They swelled and shrunk with every breath, and I watched them from the corner of my eye, almost like I was spying on us.

"Have you ever written a letter?" she asked.

"No."

"Never?"

"No."

"Well. If everything changes tomorrow, and I don't see you very much, will you write me some?"

"Okay."

"That sounded unsure."

"I'll do it."

"I'll just want to know what you're up to. You can tell me what you did that day, or something you saw. Or you can tell me something John Frederick said or write the words to a song he sang."

"I can do that."

"I like the way you put your words together. Do you think it's different because you were quiet for so long?"

"Maybe."

"Do you like talking this much?"

"I haven't decided yet."

"I've caught myself sounding like you," she said. "Some of the things I've said are the way you would say them."

"I'm sorry."

"Your lips are purple," she said. And she touched them with her finger. "The wine."

Her eyes fell then and we lay there breathing. The strength of her hands surprised me. I wanted to tell her that we had to stick together. I knew it the way an animal knows things. But she fell asleep before I could think of a way to say it.

12.

IN THE MORNING NOTHING MATTERED TO ME. ALL OF THE HIGH, FANCY feelings were gone. I made the bed, then stared at it like I would at some fish before throwing it back in the pond.

Haley and Gid were at the kitchen table. They hushed when I walked in. Then Gid said, "My wife went and got us some more muffins. They're in the bag yonder."

I poured some coffee and didn't bother heating the milk. The coffee was cold. They looked at each other, then Haley got up and left.

I drank the coffee and waited for Gid to start talking. He didn't have to say anything, but I knew he thought different. His mouth opened several times but nothing came out. I got up and poured the coffee until the grains ran in.

Finally he said, "I've made us into stray dogs and now the old man's sick."

The muffins had made the paper bag sweat. I ripped it where it was wet and took a crumb of brown sugar and put it in my coffee. Then I drank it down and coughed a little on the grit. I left him there and went outside. In the driveway I took a seat against the garage door and peeled some bark from a stick. I thought that if we went to a big town on the coast we could blend in. I could work a job and we could all live cheap. And the girl would keep a secret. And if she visited some, fine. Gid didn't need a judge to tell him he was guilty. He was acting crazy. We could live together, the three of us, and we could eat fish every night. And if the girl came down to see us, it'd be okay.

Haley found me. She sat down and hooked her arm in mine.

"What are you thinking about?"

"I'm not."

"Gid's only looking out for you."

"It's a hell of a time to start."

"Merit. We need to take John Frederick to the hospital. He's not saying anything and he has a fever. He peed in the chair last night, and he hasn't gotten up."

I scratched at the stick. It was damp and I pulled little strings from it.

"Gid said something this morning. He said, 'It's me or the old man.'"

"He's not thinking clearly," I said.

"He wants you to help him get John Frederick in my car."

"Aren't you cold out here? You might get sick too."

"He wants you to come help him," she said again.

"What do you want me to do?"

She didn't say anything, but she lessened her grip on my arm. I tossed the stick in the yard and went inside. I found Gid sitting in the chair beside the old man.

"He says it's all right for us to take him to the doctor," Gid said.

The dried piss smelt like snakes.

"He's gonna be fine. I told him that you'd stay with him."

"Just got a winter bug," the old man said.

We stood on either side of his chair. Gid bent down and pulled the lever so that the old man sat up slowly. We took him by his arms and helped him to his feet. His skin burned in my hands as the blanket that had covered him fell to his feet. I kicked it out of the way and we took him down the steps. We slipped his shoes on him at the kitchen door and met Haley in the driveway.

I sat in the back with Gid. The big houses went by and I didn't think about nothing. The car was quiet except for the heater. And we left Mountain Brook because there are never hospitals in the nicer parts of town. We rolled down the hill towards the city, and out of the cave-like stillness, over the gray hum of the car, the old man's voice came like a thing on fire.

Kick your shoes off Moses,
Do you know where you stand?
Kick your shoes off Moses,
Do you know where you stand?
Oh, kick your shoes off,
Do you know where you stand?

And he sang it over and over, stopping sharp at the end of each line to take another breath. And though the song was a circle, it seemed to build on itself. Like it was leading somewhere. He grew louder and louder, and deeper and darker, like he was angry, like he had some kind of holy authority. And when he drew another breath, my hair stood up on my arms.

When he stopped, I realized that we were in the right lane going very slow. Haley brought us back to speed. Gid looked at me with high eyebrows. We exited the highway and made our way downtown.

"Junior," Gid said. "I made a call this morning and told the law I'd be coming down. I asked would they let you and the preacher here go to the hospital so he can get better. I told them that I didn't want people to bother y'all or any damn newspaperman to get within a mile of you. They said that'd be fine."

So we drove to the courthouse. It wasn't far. We parked at the back of the lot, far away from the doors.

"Some boy's coming to give you an escort," Gid said. He was quiet. The car was hot. Then he said, "A lot of time before I beat myself for things that weren't real. Someone even told me that they heard she had her pipes tied up. But I never even asked her. Just made myself feel like a queer for not getting her pregnant."

"Okay," he said. "I got to walk up them steps. Hop out, Junior."

We got out. Gid thanked Haley, and through the open window, she kissed his cheek. Then he went around to John Frederick and asked him to look after me. They shook hands.

We stood behind the car. I didn't think about Florida or the beach. I wanted him to get it over with. We stood there with our hands in our pockets. I looked at my shoes and thought of the Wal-Mart. And how we had a pocket of money then. It seemed like a few bad years had gone by and when he walked away they would close up like a book and blow off like a storm and I would let out a long, stale breath. We stood there for a minute or more. He spit on a line. I aimed and did the same.

Finally he said, "I used to tighten all the jars in the cabinets just so she'd have to ask me to help her."

"I used to spray her underwear drawer with pesticide," I said.

He smiled and slapped the back of my head and we stood there. We pulled away and shook hands.

"Let that girl be nice to you. She's one of the good ones," he said.

"Look me up when you bust out of there."

He turned then and started across the parking lot. And I laughed at the squatty way he walked. One-eighth Indian. Then the girl was beside me. She sat on the bumper. Gid disappeared as he walked between the cars, and for a second I wondered if he had chickened out and hidden beneath a van. But I saw him again as he went up the courthouse steps. Two officers were by the door. They straightened up as he reached the top. And for a few seconds they just stared at each other. Gid turned around and waved to us. And the one officer hooked a cuff on his waving hand. But they were gentle with him. They took him inside.

The girl put her hand on my back.

"It's all right," I said.

"Excuse me y'all," a man said behind us. It was an officer in green and brown. "I'm Deputy Al Harris. I understand you have a sick friend. I'll be glad to show y'all the way to the hospital. I got it all set up so there won't be any waiting around when we get there."

We stared at him. He seemed nervous. Then he came up with his hand out. "Merit," he said. "Al Harris."

I shook his hand and said, "All right, Al. Thanks for your help."

It was like I had cussed him. He pulled back so fast. Then he gathered himself.

"Hi miss."

"Haley."

"Pleasure. So I'm parked across the street. I'll pull around and y'all can follow me."

John Frederick was asleep. The deputy pulled around and we followed him down the city streets.

"Nice man," Haley said.

"Nice enough. But I think I scared him somehow."

She looked at me in the rearview mirror and said, "Do you want me to stay with you at the hospital?"

"Yeah. If you want to."

"I do."

"Do you have to go to work tonight?"

"I already called in sick."

We pulled up to the emergency room. I noticed then that several police cars had followed. The deputy helped me get John Frederick out of the car. We walked him to the ER, but when the doors slid open, he pulled back.

"Mr. Merit," he said. "Would you take off my hat?"

We went past all of the waiting patients to another door where two other officers and a nurse stood. They all smiled at us. But as we started through, the nurse stopped Haley and said, "Ma'am, only one person can go back with him."

Haley looked at me and I looked at the nurse.

"What the hell difference does it make," I said.

The officers looked at each other. We all went on through.

Doctor Wallace came up then and introduced himself. He put his hands on John Frederick's neck and looked him in the eyes.

"I think you're gonna be fine, pal," he said.

We went up an elevator. They took us to a room where there were several beds but no other patients. We turned around while they got him in a gown. He was saying, "Oh yeah, I always want to be in the choir." He looked like a hunchbacked angel.

"Have you been eating?" the doctor asked him.

"I neber drink a beer."

"He's had a little," Haley said. "Part of a muffin and some warm milk yesterday. And a little soup. Nothing today."

"Okay. We're gonna hook you up to some nutrients. It will help you get your strength back."

"That's right."

They put the needles in him. The doctor asked us some more questions and we answered as best we could. He had to do some checks so we went out in the hall.

"He seems a little better," Haley said.

"Yeah. He likes the attention."

"The doctor's being sweet to him."

"Do you think they'll let us nap on those other beds?"

"Yeah. And I brought you Morgan's pajama pants."

The deputy came walking up.

"I wanted to tell you, Merit, that I've been reading about y'all. I know you ain't had it easy, but you got a hell of a story. I'm sorry it had to end like this."

I nodded.

"When we got the call this morning, I requested to escort y'all down here."

"Thank you."

"I know you're worn out, and I'm not gonna let any reporter get near you. But is there anything you want me to say on your behalf?"

"Just make something up."

He nodded and walked off. Haley wrapped her arms around me and squeezed my arms to my side. "Did I sound like that guy when I met you?"

"No."

"Promise?"

"A little."

"Poor guy hates his job."

The doctor motioned us back in the room. We stood around John Frederick. He had a sheet pulled up to his chest. The doctor explained that, except for a fever, the old man was healthy. He said some medicine would help bring it down, and that he wanted to keep him there until he got his strength back. Probably a day or two. While he talked, John Frederick stared at the nurse.

"We'll get him some solid food too," he said. "He told me he likes vegetables. That's why he's in such good shape."

He told us to let him rest. When the nurses left, we decided to sandwich John Frederick with a couple of extra beds. We lay on either side of him and turned the TV off.

"What was your wife's name?" Haley asked him.

"Lorna Doone. She got the way of a peacock."

"What's that mean?"

"It mean that people stop when they see her in the road. Yes sir. They stop and say 'Look out! There's the woman we been looking for.' And they roll by slow so the dust don't fly on her."

"How'd you tell her you loved her?" I baited him.

"With honey from the comb and amen singing." He said it so loud. We all laughed. "That's right. And if she get angry with me, I tell her I try better. And she say, 'John Frederick. You doing fine. Why don't you rock me a little while like you know how.' And we close the door and don't come out till Sunday."

"What'd you do when she disappeared?" she asked.

"On that day I waited by the window. And then the next day I borrow a car and go looking. And I stop at ebery station along the way and say, 'My name is John Frederick Templeton White, and I'm looking for Miss Lorna Doone Nail White. Hab anyone seen her come this way?' No one saw her come or go. So I said, 'I do thank you for your time,' and I went on to the next town. And when I run out of money, people let me take fuel for free because I tell them what I was dribing for."

We waited for a second to see if he would go on. When he didn't, I said, "John Frederick, is Verner Nail your sister-in-law?"

"That's right."

Haley looked at me. I shrugged.

"John Frederick," she asked. "Why don't you sound angry about it?"

"No sir. Not anymore."

"But why not?"

"I won't be no Israelite in the desert, crying 'Please, Moses, take us back to Egypt. Let us be slaves again.' I keep following until I cross that riber."

Maybe Haley knew what he was talking about. She said, "I want to be like you."

He put his hand on hers.

"You doing fine."

We talked into the afternoon. It was nice in there. A nurse brought us lunch. It was baked chicken and mashed potatoes with brown gravy, green beans, yellow corn, and applesauce. But the food had no taste. One plate would have been enough for all of us.

Haley took our plates when we were done. We sat there and watched John Frederick start to nod off. Then the doctor came in.

"How was your lunch?"

No one answered.

"Merit, I'm gonna need you to slide your bed over so I can get in here for a minute."

I hopped down and rolled it back a little.

"Ninety-nine point six," he said. "That fever's coming down already. Do you feel any better?"

"I don't lib on bread."

"Oh yeah? All right. Hey. I forgot to ask you. With the game coming up this weekend, are you an Auburn man or an Alabama man?"

"Yes sir. I used to lib below Auburn."

"Oh yeah?" the doctor said. "I went to UAB for school, but I'm from Maryland. I try to stay neutral. I just want it to be close."

"All right."

The doctor said a nurse would check on us after supper, and he'd be back in the morning. We looked at each other when the door shut.

"I don't like him," she said.

"I know."

We whispered while John Frederick napped between us.

"How are you feeling?" she asked.

"Fine."

"He seems better, right?"

"Yeah."

"Have you thought at all about what y'all will do when you leave here?"

"Buy a big boat."

"Good," she whispered. "Where will you sail it?"

"All ober."

"That's nice. Do you want to watch the news tonight?"

"No."

"Don't talk so much," she said. "I can't keep up."

"I don't know what we'll do when we leave here. I guess we'll go back to his trailer, and maybe I'll build a little place on his land. But I don't know. I keep having this idea of living by the sea. I could work on an oil rig, or be a longshoreman, or something like that.

They make good money and I could pay for a little place for the two of us. But I don't know."

"Don't do that," she said.

"Why not?"

"You're better than that."

I looked at her.

"What?" she said. "I mean that. I wish someone would say something to me for being a twenty-one-year-old bartender who lives with her mom."

The machines were beeping.

"Why should they?" I said after a while. "Why should they say something to you? We do what we have to do."

"I guess," she said.

We sat there for a long time. There was a picture on the wall of an orange sunset. It was a nice picture, but it seemed like a hell of a thing to hang in a hospital room.

We both opened our mouths at the same time.

"You first," I said.

"No. I talk all the time."

"I was just thinking about all those slaves who found out they were free and just went about their chores."

"Yeah?"

"And I was wondering if you'd really move away if everything got better at home."

Her chin was on her breastbone and her hands were folded between her legs. "Oh," she said.

"What were you going to say?"

"I was just going to say I'm sorry. There's nothing wrong with you working on an oil rig. I just don't want you to be that far away. That was a terrible thing I said. I sounded like my parents."

"You know you could come and visit. I'm thinking of buying up most of the beachfront and kicking everybody out. It'll be nice and quiet."

"Merit," she said. "Have you ever been to the beach?"

"No. But I've found a lot of prehistoric shark teeth in the creek."

"How do you know you'll like it?"

"How do you know you'll like living in a tree?"

After a while I rolled a fourth bed up against hers.

13.

We sat on the air conditioner and put our hands on the glass. It was cold out there. Down below an ambulance pulled up with its lights on. But there was no siren so I didn't worry about the patient. They were either dead already or not in that bad of shape.

"What do you want to do tonight?" she said.

"I don't know. Do you think they'll let Gid call?"

"I don't think so."

"Do you think they have wine in the cafeteria?"

"No."

"Maybe the deputy will get us some," I said. "You ask him. He likes you."

"Merit. We can't drink in the hospital."

"Oh."

"There's my work," she said and pointed outside.

We could just see the place with our foreheads on the window.

"Were those Christmas lights there before?" I asked.

"They're always up."

"Did you know it was us when we walked in?"

"Yeah."

"But nobody else did?"

"Most people don't notice things."

"Let's go down there and get some whiskey."

"You want a double?"

"Yeah."

Our dinner came then and we sat on either side of John Frederick.

"Do you got any beer?" I asked the nurse.

She was embarrassed. She left.

"She likes you Merit," Haley said. "Maybe you should come down sick. You could let her take care of you."

"She's got a rock," I said, and pointed to my finger.

She rolled her eyes.

"John Frederick," she said. "Did you sleep all right?"

"I dream I was sleeping beneath an apple tree and my wife come and wake me up. And she pick an apple for me to eat. So I sit up and take a bite."

He was quiet, so she said, "That's all?"

"Yes ma'am. Only one bite."

The macaroni and cheese wasn't that bad. It had more salt than the ham. And the pineapple cake was okay. But I was glad that John Frederick was still hooked up to the bag. It wasn't a meal to get your legs back.

"When you feel well enough to leave," she asked him, "where do you think you and Merit should go?"

"I feel good."

"But do you think it would be good to go back to your trailer, or do you want to live somewhere else?"

"No city keeps on. How 'bout that? And that's for a town too. And eben a home."

She thought for a minute then said, "Have you ever been to the beach?"

"I neber been oberseas. No ma'am."

There could be no planning with John Frederick. He could only think about the moment he was hunched in, or about the great beyond. You couldn't start reasoning with him about anything. He had gotten to the bottom of all of it and forgotten how he got there.

"Tell her about your mule," I said.

"You want to hear about my plow mule?" he said.

"Tell her. I've heard it before."

"Okay. Let me remember about it. All right. Yes sir. I call that mule Coffee Brown. He hab one lazy eye and one white shoe. And ebery day he work without grumbling for thirteen years. But no Sundays. And one day the newspaper come and take a picture of him with the she-goat that belong to my cousin's wife. And I cut out the picture to show it to him. And I hold it up to each eye because I'm neber sure which one work the best. He look at it and he knew it was him. But he stay true and work just as hard the next day. He libed on till Nobember and one morning he didn't wake up. So I take what money I hab and get a tractor."

"But tell her why they took the picture of him," I said.

"Oh," he said. "The goat that belong to my cousin's wife was named Regina. And she decide that Coffee Brown was a prince. When the work get done and my mule got done sweating and eat his grain and drink some water, she walk up to him and pick her front hoof off the ground. When she do that, he settle down to the ground and lay with his legs out behind him and his belly on the earth. Regina would climb up on his back and stand watch ober the field. Then she would settle down too and lay on his back and take a nap. Coffee Brown neber minded it. I don't know if he slept too because I can't tell."

"So the newspaper got a picture of them like that?" she asked.

"Yes ma'am. But not the first try. That man try to walk right up and click one, but if the she-goat see anyone coming, she hop off until the next day. So the next day he come back and stay on the other side of the field. And he juke a gyroscope on the end of his camera so he could make it up close."

"Did you bury Coffee Brown?" she asked.

"No. I burn him."

She flinched a little, then said, "Did you like having a tractor more?"

"They both good. But the mule is a better animal because he's quiet and you can hear the earth turn and squeak. And you can hear the thunder when it still a long way off. And if it be eben further away, you know it be on its way because you watch his ears. The mule is better too because you can talk to him all day. Some mens will talk to their tractors but they really talking to themselves. When I was behind a mule or an ox, I talk to God some and I talk to the animal some. And sometimes I talk to both at the same time. God and the mule."

It didn't matter what he talked about. There was a melody in it that I'm always trying to remember. But Haley had to know what he meant. After a minute she asked him, "John Frederick. How do you know God hears you?"

"I know he does," he said. "Sometime you talk to someone but they don't listen. They neber ask you anything about the things you say. But God ask me things all the time. I tell him one thing and he listen and think it ober. Then he ask me something about it."

"I see," she said. "But you didn't ask him why your wife disappeared?"

"Yes I did," he said. "And I ask him if he help me find her. And I told him I was sad about it and that I like to die instead of her. But I know that I lib in a place that's broke. And I know it's gonna stay broke until the man comes back to smooth out all the rough places. Ebery morning I wonder if it be the day. And I say 'Amen. Come Lord Jesus.' And when I go to sleep and eberything still broke, and I still don't know where she went or if she dead, I don't curse God because he ain't the one who made this place get sick. He just the one who's gonna get it well. So I wait up."

He slept again. His temperature was almost normal. We'd get to leave soon. Get to go on back to his place, back to regular. And I couldn't sit still. I started messing with the controls on my bed.

"I thought you never got restless."

"Me too."

14.

SHE WAS AT THE WINDOW. HER TANGLED HAIR. HER LONG BACK AND HER legs. Her forehead was on the glass and her breath clouded the glass. I took a few steps towards her and slid the rest of the way on my socks. I was behind her. She pulled me beside her and held onto my arm.

"Do you think I should gain some weight?" I said.

"How would you do that, Merit?"

I looked at us in the window.

"I'm tired," she said. "My parents get back Saturday."

"Have you talked to them?"

"Yeah. They don't know anything."

"What would they say?"

She didn't answer.

"What day is it now?" I asked.

"Tuesday."

There were some blankets on a chair. I put one over John Frederick, and pulled the bottom up so that his feet showed. We got in one of the beds and lay there talking.

After a while I jerked.

"Merit," she whispered. "You fell asleep. Your pajama pants are in the bag."

I didn't get up.

"Should I turn the light off?" she said.

"No," I said, and pulled the blanket over our heads.

"This hospital's not much fun," she said. "Tomorrow we'll smuggle some wine."

———

I don't remember what I dreamed. I only remember feeling warm. There was some kind of innocence in it. I could have been standing in a warm rain. Or I could have been rolling in some high grass beside the water. I'm not sure. But it was like I was allowed to laugh without memory. Like I had just been born a laughing baby. I get cold when I think about it now. The girl said the same thing happened to her. She tried to tell me about it but didn't know how.

"Merit." She shook me. "What's that?"

The old man was groaning. We lay very still. He got louder. But I didn't pull the blanket away. Then, after maybe a minute, he began to speak.

"One day I walk in the earth before the sun make the sky, and the dark was weak, and the dirt was warm on top but cool on the underside. And I wear no shoes so I can feel it. The sun was coming and I don't mind, but I want to keep the dirt coming cool in my toes. I was a young man, and eberyone I know want a house and a Sunday suit. And I want those things just like them, but I want another thing too. I want the dirt to stay cool under my feet. So I wake up first and I walk the field and I get angry that the ground will cook again. I get angry more and more that the whole day can't be dawn. Then one morning I say I'm gonna stand in one place for the whole day long with my feet buried deep where it's cold and I stay there all day with it like that and I don't work like eberybody else.

"When the day arribe they see me in the place I find and they come and say it's time to work, and what do I want standing there with no shoes? But I keep my eyes closed and I keep feeling where it's cool. They go to work and I stay there and it start to get hot. It was still morning but my hat was in the house and the sun made me think inside up. I mobe my toes to feel but I can't tell if they cold or hot. I think hard about it and try to feel down there. But then I fall out and they find me and carry me to the house.

"When I got better eberbody say I'm not right for standing out like that. But they all doing the same as me and I know it. They all want a Sunday suit with a fancy stripe and they want that suit to neber get worn and to always look their best. I learn then that it neber be that way. And I stop trying to make heaben come to south Georgia before it supposed to. I start to wait.

"And I wait up and I work. Nothing make me afraid anymore. I don't worry about the sun or the rain. Or what I eat or the kind of shoes on my feet. Death puts a shadow on eberyone I see. But it don't put one on me because I look at Glory. So I go on for seventy-four years and life bends me ober like a reed and my eyes turn like an alligator's. And I watch people get sick and when they die their family don't come to church anymore. And I know a boy who gib his last sixty-three cents for a cup of gasoline and pour it on his hair and light himself in the street. And I know his daddy just went walking and neber come back. But I go on and I see a thousand black men and women walk down the road and they say they going to Montgomery for justice, and would I like to come? But I say I stay by my field because there be no one to water my mule and because heaben ain't in Montgomery, Alabama. And I find a woman in a bean patch with hair like a rain cloud and I tell her if her hair fall out, I lub her anyway. And we walk in the cool dirt in the morning before I go to work. Then one day I come in and she's gone. But I go on and I wait up. And if something hurt my body, I say, 'I know. I know I'm gonna hurt as long as I'm here.' But I look down the line and I take another step. And sometimes I groan because I start to think that she just went away. And I say, 'I know. I know I'm gonna groan.' And I bend like a reed under all of it but I've heard about the weight of Glory. So I wait up for that day when all things become new. When the night be like day but the sun don't beat upon us and the one who is coming wipes all the tears out of eberybody's eyes. Then shall we go from strength to strength, and from glory to glory, and no one gets tired, and no one beats his breast, and the hound lies with the coon.

"Amen. All right. Okay. Yeah," he said quietly. "All right. That's right."

Then we just heard him breathing. It got calmer and calmer until, finally, he snored. I opened my eyes then and the girl was looking at me. We lay there listening to him for a long time.

15.

IN THE MORNING HE NEVER WOKE UP. I KNEW IT WHEN I LOOKED AT HIM.
His hands were folded on his chest.

I told the people to bury him anyplace. I told them that he didn't
need a funeral because there was no one who could talk about him.

We moved to another room. They let Gid call. He sounded bad.
But he told me two things. He said that when he was facedown on
her brother's floor thinking he was good for nothing, thinking that
he couldn't even be a jealous lover and kill a man who had his pants
around his feet, the old man had wandered in and found him. He
had stood over him for too long, and it was making Gid angry. And
then the old man had gone in the bathroom and filled a cup of
water and come back and poured it on Gid. And Gid had hopped
up and said that he was a smelly old nigger who was trying to steal
his son. And John Frederick had said that Gid could hit him if he
wanted, so long as he quit beating himself up. That was one thing.

The other was a talk the two of them had when I was with the
girl at the golf course. Gid had asked him why he had let me hang
around all those years. And John Frederick told him that the day I
first came was the day he turned sixty-six. And that was the only day
he'd ever lay in bed all morning. When he finally got up, he thought
he could ride his tractor for a while. But it wouldn't start. And he
said it was like the whole world had rolled up on his shoulders, and

he asked God if he could go inside and help himself to die and go on to heaven. So he was walking back to his trailer and his hat blew off and he thought he wouldn't need it anymore. So he kept on. And I had run up beside him and handed him the thing. And then, like a great bird had come down and hooked his talons in it, the weight was gone.

After Gid had told me that, he sounded better. He asked to speak to the girl. The phone was loud and I could hear what he was saying. He told her he caught John Frederick's cough and was treating it with vanilla pudding. It made her smile.

We stayed another night but we lay in separate beds. We talked very late and I told her all of the good stories I know. I didn't want her to worry.

In the morning she went and talked to the hospital people. I put cold water on my face. Then I changed my socks.

16.

WE DROVE OUT OF BIRMINGHAM AGAINST THE MORNING TRAFFIC. OUT
280 past a thousand fancy strip malls. We caught most of the lights
and took it easy. There was a big hill, and at the top, I saw the town
in the mirror. I put my feet up on the dash and listened to the
motor.

She turned off the highway and we kept south on the little
roads. We were in the country then. The trees had shed the last of
their leaves in the storm. The grass was dead. I tried to set the little
houses I saw against the ones from Mountain Brook. To set the
classes shoulder to shoulder. I wondered who was happier. Then I
remembered that it was her and me in the same car, shoulder to
shoulder, and happiness seemed like a little thing to try and meas-
ure. Who had a lot of it?

I liked the way she drove. Every curve was smooth and easy,
and she didn't mind the pale yellow line. I wished that we could go
on like that for hours—the heat on our feet and the back window
cracked a little and the radio barely loud enough to hear. She was
all right.

The roads rolled out before us like ribbons. A couple of weeks
before she could have driven one and seen three guys shuffling by.
Maybe I would have waved to her. Maybe Gid would have told her
to stay on her side of the damn road.

"Merit?" she said.

"What?"

"Will you be okay by yourself for a few days?"

"Yeah."

"You won't run off?" she looked at me. "You'll call me if you get antsy?"

"I'm just gonna hibernate."

"Good."

"What are you gonna do?"

"I'll sit my parents down and tell them what's happened. I'm not looking forward to that. I'll work tomorrow night and Friday night, but I'll try to take off Saturday and come back down here."

"What will we do when you come back?"

But she just drove. I looked out the window at the trailers with their junk and their stairs without handrails, then back at the girl. Her eyes were barely open.

"Hey," I said.

She laughed and rubbed her hand across her face.

"Ohhh," she said. "You won't come live in Birmingham for a little while? I could find you a good job and an apartment."

I folded my arms on the dash and watched the pavement. Soon we were by the lake. We crossed the dam and turned off into a neighborhood. The houses were big again and they sat on the water. In the driveway she opened a box and punched in a code that opened the gate. Then she parked outside the garage. We opened our doors, but for a while neither of us would get out. Then, when the car had gotten cold, I slipped my shoes on. She got the bag out of the backseat.

We walked around the front of the house. She stopped on the path. I waited for her.

"I don't have the keys," she said. "They're at home."

"All right."

She went to the steps and sat. I picked a wet walnut out of the grass and tossed it at a tree. Then I found another and hit the neighbor's driveway.

"I don't have to stay here," I said.

"You'll stay here. But I don't know if I should go back and get the keys or if I should just break a window. I'm not sure if I could find the keys if I did go home."

"Is there an alarm?"

"No."

I sat beside her. She put her hand on my shoulder and said, "If I choose the window, will you break it?"

I found a nice rock from beneath a shrub. Around back, below the deck, was a sliding door. She was staring at it and I started to laugh.

"Bad idea?" she said.

"C'mon," I said, and took her arm and led her up the steps.

I found a regular window and took my stance. Then I put the rock through. It was loud. She laughed. My hand started to sting and then the blood came. I unlocked the window, opened it, and climbed through. Blood dripped on the sill. I put my wrist in my overalls to keep it off the carpet. Then I unlocked the door.

Blood and water mixed in the sink. We cut a towel and wrapped the cuts.

"Sorry," she said.

"It's fine."

"Does it need stitches?"

"No."

We sat on the couch and talked. She told me she liked it better at the lake house in the fall and winter. Then you could walk down to the dock in a big quilt and watch the way the wind combed the water without some ski boat messing up the pattern. She told me that she liked the water but she didn't like going out on it. They had dammed the river to make it years ago, and she couldn't help but think of all the yards where kids used to play, now only the muddy bottom of a lake.

"Look at the water," she said. "It looks like a blanket fort has fallen on a bunch of children. And they're all trying to crawl out from it. You can pick one and follow it all the way to the shore."

I got up and sat on the other side of her so she could have my good hand. Her knee stuck out from the tear in her jeans and she put my hand there.

"You gonna be okay?"

"Yeah," I said. "I'm just gonna rest."

"You think Gid did the right thing now?"

"I guess so."

"I mean the timing."

"Yeah."

"It would have been bad if he would have waited even one more day."

"It's pretty bad as it is."

"I'm sorry."

"It's okay. Gid will be fine in there. He likes being taken care of."

"I am sorry though."

Then she wouldn't say much. The wind made a queer whistle through the broken glass. I tried to get her to dream. I said what about going west? Maybe not live up in a tree, but I could build her a cabin with a tree growing through it. Or we could go to the sea. We could get out of Alabama next week, or the week after. But she couldn't talk about it. She said we should think about everything separately for a few days, then iron it out when she came back. She said we should figure out what was best for me.

We were quiet for a long time. Her hands were folded in her lap. All I finally said was, "Do you need to be going now?"

"I think so."

I got up and walked into the kitchen. There was a dull pounding in my hand.

"There's a lot of canned food in the pantry," she said. "And here's some money if you need anything."

I went to her.

"I'll see you, Merit."

I fogged the leaded glass on the front door. She turned out and drove off pretty fast. I went outside in my socks. The ground was damp. I picked another walnut out of the grass, squished the shell, and rubbed the black, felty stuff into my good hand. Two squirrels ran around and around a tree. One was chasing the other. They raced from twig to twig.

17.

A MOCKINGBIRD FLEW IN THROUGH THE WINDOW TODAY. HE MADE A LOT of noise and knocked into a couple walls. I opened all the windows and doors. But he sat up on a bookshelf and hollered at me. I yelled at him. He yelled back. It seemed like a good game. I yelled again, and we went back and forth for a few minutes. He was a cocky thing. I threw a pillow at him. That got him going louder. I went in the bathroom and hoped he would leave. I found a razor, turned the water on, and waited for it to run hot. Then I shaved my mustache. When I came out, he had left. Or maybe he went upstairs. Anyway, I haven't seen him again.

Two days of sitting around. I can see twenty years play out before me in a minute. Then I can come back and do it all different- ly. It was better when I was content to kick my feet and bump around. When I didn't care that the future was forested. But the girl taught me to climb the tallest tree and look out. She said my name. She fed me. She looked at me long and even until it seemed I was coming to life. And maybe I did, because today, time has a handle on me. I make plans now. But I can't keep the shadows off.

Every time the heater cuts on, I think it's her car door. It's hap- pened a dozen times today, but it gets me still. Earlier I tried to make a list of the reasons we should stick together, just in case she's con- fused. All I could think of was this: she gets things the same way I do. The things that make sense to me make sense to her, and the stuff that's too damn confusing for me is the same for her.

Auburn beat Alabama. The game ended a while ago, 28-23. Half the state is happy. The other half gets to feel that, for one night, the only thing wrong is a football score. Cadillac Williams thanked the Lord. I wonder if he talks to God like John Frederick did. I wonder if he'll still be happy if he tears his knee up and he can't ever play again. Happy or not, I hope it doesn't happen. I like to watch him go. He runs like hell's after him, like if he doesn't bust free, someone's gonna do something bad to his family.

Somewhere in the third quarter I had an idea to get drunk. All rich people have a liquor cabinet, and I figured I'd find a bottle and warm up with it. I headed for the kitchen but was stopped by a largemouth bass mounted on the wall. It had fake yellow eyes, about the color of John Frederick's. I imagined that if the old man was around, he would grab me by the hand and tell me something crazy, something to settle me. He had more cause to drink than I did. And I remembered the doctor saying he was the only old black man he had ever seen with perfect blood pressure. That he had no medical reason to die. I looked at that fish again, wondering what good reason the old man ever had to live. His shoes were in my bag. I turned away from the kitchen and went to find them. I slipped the things on and shuffled back and forth. And I thought of his feet down there in the cool dirt.

ACKNOWLEDGMENTS

I am very grateful for my parents, and for J. MacKenzie, Hayes, L.N. Fairley, B.A., Rick, Sonny, Karan, Hal Foster, Nate and C.B., B.J. Webber, Dr. Timothy J. Keller, The Anniston Star and for all of you who sat in my living room on Wednesday nights.